Flight of the

Dragon Kyn

BOOKS BY SUSAN FLETCHER

Dragon's Milk
The Stuttgart Nanny Mafia
Flight of the Dragon Kyn

Flight of the
Dragon Kyn

SUSAN FLETCHER

A Jean Karl Book
Atheneum Books for Young Readers

Atheneum Books for Young Readers
An imprint of Simon & Schuster Children's Publishing Division
1230 Avenue of the Americas
New York, New York 10020

Library of Congress Cataloging-in-Publication Data
Fletcher, Susan, 1951–
Flight of the Dragon Kyn / Susan Fletcher. — 1st ed.
p. cm.
"A Jean Karl book."
Summary: Fifteen-year-old Kara is summoned by King Orrik, who
believes she has the power to call down the dragons that have been
plundering his realm, and she is caught up in the fierce rivalry
between Orrik and his jealous brother Rog.
ISBN 0-689-31880-4
[1. Fantasy. 2. Dragons—Fiction. 3. Kings, queens, rulers,
etc.—Fiction.] I. Title.
PZ7.F6356F1 1993
[Fic]—dc20 92-44787

FIRST EDITION
Printed in the United States of America
10 9 8 7
The text of this book is set in Garamond #3.
Book design by Claire Naylon Vaccaro

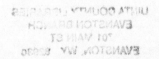

For Mom and Dad

I gratefully acknowledge the generous help of falconers Byron Gardner and Bob Welle. Many thanks, as well, to Dave Siddon, Cathi Wright, and Deanna Sawtelle from Portland, Oregon's, Metropolitan Zoo. I am indebted to Jim Todd, from the Oregon Museum of Science and Industry, for moving the sun and moon to help me; and to Hakan Carheden for insight into Scandinavia.

Chapter 1

*A prodigious gift
trails peril in its wake.*

—KRAGISH

FOLK SAYING

I was fifteen in the year the king's men came to take me from
my home.

It was a lean year that portended hunger; little rain had
fallen in the summer, so the grass grew scant and the sheep
wasted thin. Many folk had marked the fleeting shadows of
dragons twisting across the fells, and a score of lambs had
vanished without trace. Then came the early frost, which
blighted our hopes for a long growing season and for fodder
to last through winter.

I was gathering angelica in the hills above the steading
when they came. I ought to have been spinning. My mother
and my aunt and my brothers' wives all said so. *They* were
spinning—in the smoke-dense gloom of the hearthroom
house, their spindles whirring drearily, the only hint of light

the thin yellow haze that sifted down from the smokehole. It's too late for angelica, they all said; it's gone by now; best you stay here and make yourself useful, for a change.

But I knew of secret places in the hills—sheltered nooks where the sun warmed the earth and the wind couldn't pry in to chill it—and I said that I could find some.

My mother relented, as usual. My brothers' wives scolded her for cosseting me; my aunt said I was lazy and ill-mannered and strange.

I didn't care; I was gone.

It was one of those clear, frosty days when the wind snaps your cloak and fleets of clouds scud like warships across the sky. The sun lay low about the mountains, piercing the air with shafts of liquid light that glittered on the fjord and haloed the rime-shaggy firs. I breathed in deep, savoring this place. Up here in the hills above the steading was the only place where I was free to live my own life, untrammeled by disapproval and suspicion. Before long, I had found four small clumps of angelica—shriveled, perhaps, but they would yet lend fragrance to the strew-reeds, and their roots were still potent for balm.

A whitchil called from a hawthorn tree; I called back. It swooped down and landed on my wrist, eyeing me unabashed, its fierce little claws pricking my skin. I called down a gull, too, which landed on my elbow, and a crake, and a sleepy stony owl that tucked one foot up and tried to take a nap on my arm. "Wake up," I said, twisting my arm so they all lost their balance and clutched me and wildly flapped their wings.

I laughed and stroked them one by one. My father had forbidden me to call down birds, so I did it away from the steading, where no one could see. I kept my left arm well covered to hide the scratches, but I know my father knew. I know *everyone* knew, from the way their eyes slid away from mine when I returned, from the whispers behind my back when my mother and father were not near. Whispers of my old illness, and how it had changed me. Whispers of dragons . . .

Gently I ruffled the feathers on the stony owl's breast, calming my mind. When I looked up again, I caught a movement—a glinting—in the valley below. I shielded my eyes to mark what it was.

There, far down in the rime-crusted folds of the valley, came five moving *things*—no, six, or seven, perhaps.

A chill gust of wind breathed on my face and whuffed in my ears; a jingling of bells drifted up.

Horsemen. They were horsemen; I could see that now. And before them moved something—something light-hued and hard to pick out from the frost.

Through the rattle of fell fronds rose yet another sound, a plaintive bleating of sheep.

Sheep!

Who would come now, on horseback, driving sheep?

Quickly I pulled up the bits of angelica I'd found—my trophies, my proofs. I tucked them under my sash and scrambled down the hillside. Pebbles clattered and slid beneath my feet. The crake and the seabird fluttered off; the owl half-spread its wings for balance and then, giving up, soared away with a disgusted hoot. Only the whitchil stayed; bobbing its head, it sidestepped up my arm until perched upon my shoulder. When I came to the rocky outcrop that overlooks the homefields I climbed atop it and looked out.

The steading's grass-roofed buildings clustered below. Blue drifts of woodsmoke gusted in whirling eddies from the hearthroom and kitchenhouses. From here, I could see the mooring place on the fjord, and two red-sailed knarrs lying in.

Red-sailed. King's knarrs.

Never since my grandfather's youth had a king's knarr put in at our steading.

What could King Orrik want with us?

As I watched, sheep and horsemen emerged from behind a thicket of birches that rippled and silvered in the wind. They were yet small in the distance. The horses looked like elfin steeds, decked out in red and mounted by metal-helmed, crimson-caped figures. Six riders there were, and one horse riderless. And behind them two great carts filled to overflowing with something that looked like hay.

Stranger still.

My heart beat loudly in my throat. What did they want? Was there war? Did they come mustering an army?

But why the sheep?

A shout went up; men came pouring out of the smithy. I recognized my father's lank-legged stride as he approached the riders. They halted. As the lead horseman conferred with my father, maids and housecarls emerged from the stables and byres and storerooms. Two of my brothers came running from the homefields; my mother and my brothers' wives and my aunt bustled out from the hearthroom house.

I stayed to watch no more, but hastened, running, for home. With a sharp cry, the whitchil took wing. The steading sank from view behind hills and stands of trees; clouds made a shifting patchwork of light and dark upon the ground. My breath came in short, frosty puffs, and soon my nose felt numb.

When at last I reached the courtyard, it was thronged, but I could find no one there from my family. Nor did I see the strangers' horses, nor the sheep; they must have been stabled and byred. But a smoke plume arose from the hall, where great company—when we had it—was entertained. I pushed open the heavy door, thinking to slip in unnoticed and listen from a shadowed corner.

My father's voice stopped me at once.

"Ah, there she is. Kara, come here."

Beyond the light from the smokehole I saw them seated around the table: my father and my mother, the king's men, my brothers and their wives. All turned to stare at me.

My father stood and said the name of one of the king's men, who rose and turned to me. I heard "Prince" but did not grasp the meaning of the name that followed, so surprised was I that my father had stopped his dealings with these men to mark my coming. The prince said something to me, and then my father spoke to me again—about a journey, King Orrik's court, a great honor, and many sheep—but I was still too numb to understand how one thing connected to another and why he spoke of any of it to me.

"Unlike a tryst," my father said, "and yet more like an apprenticeship. You need marry no one, and you may return home to us within three years."

"I . . . don't understand," I said.

The prince, a tall, burly warrior with an unruly red beard, began to speak to me. I forced myself to listen to his words, to fit them together so that they would make sense.

King Orrik, he said, had made a vow to his lady-love, Signy—here he glanced at my father. Well, the prince continued, the substance of the vow mattered not. The king was determined to do his lady's bidding; she would not marry him else. And yet this oath was not an easy one to keep, and Orrik had need of . . . certain powers. "Powers *you* possess," he said.

"Powers?" I turned to my father, suddenly sick in my heart. Surely he would not betray me. Surely he would not let this man make use of me to attain his own ends, as those suitors had tried to do.

My father and mother exchanged looks. My aunt suppressed a smile. "He will not harm . . . your birds," my father said. "Prince Rog has sworn to that. Birds count for naught in this matter."

Prince Rog. Then this was not just one of the many larger steaders who called themselves princes. This man was Rog, the king's own younger brother.

"Then I do not see," I said—carefully, reasonably—"what use my powers, as you call them, could possibly be to the king. It is little enough, what I do, and sometimes I cannot manage it, and always it has to do with birds."

Prince Rog smiled a smile that did not reach his eyes. His teeth were crooked and yellow. His glance moved to linger upon the vermilion mark on my cheek. "All this I have told the king," he said, "but my brother would not be content until he met you for himself, to see if you might . . . be of use. And if—as I think—you cannot help in this matter, I will persuade him to send you home the sooner."

"Help?" I struggled to keep my voice calm, but what I wanted more than anything was to run, run out of this hall, run away into the hills above the steading and stay there until these men went away. "What could *I* do to help the king?"

Rog turned to my father, as if he did not wish to deal with me himself. "The king wishes only to meet her, to try. It may well be that he is mistaken about her. Indeed"—and here he lowered his voice so that only I and my father could attend him—"if I were king, I would never have come all this distance to fetch a mere girl. And I believe my brother will be of a different mind once he sets eyes upon her. She'll likely be home within a half-moon."

"The choice is yours, Kara," my father said. "Whatsoever befalls, they will treat you well."

"As the king's own kin," Rog added.

"But I don't want to leave here. You know that, my father."

Twice I had been asked for in marriage at a Gathering, even though my aunt had said no one would want a girl as strange as I. My first suitor asked me to show him the hills above the steading. He spoke to me sweetly and, after a time, asked me to call down a kestrel from the air. As the bird neared my arm, the man took out his bow and shot it dead. I refused to call birds for my second suitor; he struck me across the face.

After that I vowed never to marry: never to live far away in a strange man's home and bend to his will and that of his kin. And the king's will would be worse—more absolute, unbendable.

I wouldn't dare call down birds at the king's steading. Here, I was the steader's only daughter; I was shielded from those who despised me; I could escape to the hills. But there . . . I'd have to stay indoors—spinning, most likely. There would be no escape. And with no one to quell the whispers, they would rise to a roar.

"Kara," my father said, and I could tell by the studied gentleness in his voice that he had something hard to tell me. "You cannot live this way forever, running into the hills or to your mother for protection. This life you live here is no good for you. Perhaps a new place, being useful to the king . . ."

My heart gave a lurch. The king! How did he mean to use me? The vow . . .

"What *is* this vow the king has sworn?" I asked, unable

7

any longer to rein in my fear. "And what will he want me to do? Why don't you tell me? Even a concubine knows what is expected of her! Surely you can't—"

"It is not as a concubine you would go!" my mother burst out. "And Orrik himself has sworn to keep you safe. *Sworn* it!"

"But what is this vow? I want to know!"

Rog was looking at me through narrowed eyes; he did not answer.

"You care only for yourself!" said Ragnhild, my eldest brother's wife. "Two marriage matches you were offered, and both you refused. What are you waiting for—a prince? Or will you stay on here forever, eating up the food my babes should have? And now—with the storehouses near empty, and all of our fates in your hands—even now you refuse to go."

"Dragons' shadows on the fells!" cried Hurtla, my second brother's wife. "I saw them myself. And a score of lambs are gone. Gone! Vanished! We'll starve here without the sheep and fodder the king sent. We'll starve!"

"The sheep?" I turned to my father. "Those sheep are . . . in trade . . . for me?"

He nodded.

My plight was coming clear. If I left now with these men to do the bidding of the king—whatever that might be—then no one at our steading would go hungry come spring. The sheep would carry them through. And if I refused, and if someone—a child—were lost, they would lay it at my feet. And the fault truly *would* be mine.

I could not refuse.

And yet . . .

A secret, guilty hope fluttered up inside my chest. My mother . . . perhaps she wouldn't let me go. Wouldn't let them take me away, to a strange place, to make *use* of me for their ends. Perhaps . . .

I drew myself up. "Very well," I said. "I will go."

I waited for it, my mother's voice, calling out that it must not be.

The silence hung on; my eyes sought hers in the shadows. Her head was down; she shook silently; tears streaked down her face.

It was then that I knew my lot was cast.

After that, things happened quickly. The men rose from the table, speaking of winds and tides and the need to be under way. The women moved out the door and came back bearing silver brooches and lengths of wadmal, sealskins and reindeer pelts, and combs of walrus tusk. They were all bundled together and taken out into the courtyard, where I could hear the clopping of horses' hooves. My father embraced me first, and then my mother, sobbing, clinging, until my father touched her shoulder and she let go slowly and backed away.

Then somehow I was outside in the courtyard, with Rog and the king's hearth companions and their belled and wool-draped horses. Rog set a cape about my shoulders—a crimson wool cape of downier loft and finer weave than ever I had seen. He fastened it with a gold brooch and set a gold circlet on my brow. I mounted; we set off.

Our hoofbeats rang on the frost-hard ground. The wind ripped the hood from my head and tangled in my hair. When we came to the birch thicket, I drew up my horse and looked back.

I could hear the wind soughing in the firs, the cry of a gull overhead. The sun had disappeared behind the mountains and long shadows stretched across the vale. A billowing blue mass of clouds bulked to the east, but a single slab of light caught the grasses of the steading's turfed roofs, drenching them in brightness, silhouetting each thin blade against the mountains. As I watched, the light dimmed and was doused.

And so I left them all—my mother and my father and my brothers, the birds that I so loved to call, the fine turf-roofed houses, the mountains with their tumbling becks and falls—my birthplace, my steading, my home.

Chapter 2

Lonesome it is
when the sea-steeds toss their frothy manes
far from the home-hearth.

—K RAGISH SKALD

J ust beyond the birches, out of sight of the folk watching
from the courtyard, two young men of our band put spur
to their horses and began to make sport. They raced breakneck
down the steep, pebble-strewn track to the sea, then wheeled
about and charged straight for us, veering off in the pinch of
time. One passed me so nearly by that my own mount shied
and reared, nearly pitching me off. As it was, my gold circlet
tumbled from my head, skittered across the track, and fell
down a shallow embankment. The one who had startled my
horse leapt from his own mount and retrieved the circlet,
polishing it clean with his coat.

He was clean-shaven and differently garbed from the others. Instead of the scarlet cape and metal helm of the royal
hearth companions, he wore an open fur-trimmed coat of a cut

I had never seen, with a black fur kalat on his head. His goatskin jerkin was girded by a sash of many colors loosely intertwined, from which dangled tinkling trinkets of silver and gold. His hair was different, too: darker, and tied back at the nape by a thin leather thong.

He approached me, bowed stiffly, and held out the circlet. "Forgive me, Lady," he said, and his words sounded oddly clipped and careful, as if they were strange on his tongue. I was held for a moment by his eyes, unexpectedly long and dark above high, flat cheekbones.

Then all about us the men began to make hooting sounds and kissing sounds and ribald jibes. "Kazan," they called him, and me, "the bird girl." I snatched the circlet, my face burning. I jammed it onto my head and spurred my horse down the track. Where was Prince Rog? Surely he would not tolerate this. But when I caught sight of him just ahead, my heart sank. He was turned around in his saddle, grinning. When he caught my eye, he barked out a short, hard laugh.

Treated as the king's own kin, he had said! Those had been words only, to placate *my* kin. I was on my own, with no protection. Rog would treat with me as he pleased.

At the ship landing we dismounted, and the men coaxed the horses into the holds of the two knarrs. The long-eyed youth offered to help me aboard—bowing, again. Surely he mocked me, and yet . . . In any case, I did not want to start up the hooting and laughing again. I made my way up the shore plank hardly deigning to give him a glance.

These knarrs were broader in the beam than the one my uncle took on his expeditions north for walrus and seabirds and whales. Each had a cargo hold amidships that was open to the sky. When I stepped down into it, the fore and aft decks stood waist-high. I picked my way through the maze of casks and crates and bales, breathing in the smells of damp wool and men's sweat, of salt and pitch and horses. The hearth companions found perches wherever they could; most sat with the crew at oar. At last I settled myself in a heap of hay, as far from the others as I might.

Soon the oars were thunking rhythmically, and a fine salt spray dampened my face and hair. Snow went flurrying past, but it was thin and did not stick. Kazan, the long-eyed youth, brought me a heap of blankets and skins. I nodded briefly, then turned away and busied myself arranging a skin-and-blanket nest. I felt his lingering presence; but when at last I looked up, he had gone.

There was a boy, I saw, on board. He scurried about, feeding the horses, fetching brew for the men. From time to time I caught him eyeing me furtively. He couldn't have been much more than eight winters old. He was dressed as one highborn—in a fine striped cloak of close-woven wool—yet it was dirty and wet and hung too long about his legs.

As we drew near to the mouth of the fjord, the waves bulked larger. The oarsmen unfurled the sail, with much running and shouting and creaking of rope. The wind billowed out the canvas and pushed us through the strait; we heeled north into the open sea.

Here there was no staying dry. The knarr pitched sharply; the horses stomped and blew. I crouched in the shelter of some casks, but the waves threw up sheets of spume, leaving horses, bales, and men all dripping.

My red cloak had gone heavy and sodden; I peeled it off. Likewise, I removed the golden circlet, which had begun to pinch my forehead and make it ache. I wrapped it in the cloak and wedged it between two barrels. Then I piled the sheepskins over me to make a tent of sorts and huddled, shivering, inside.

At last we put in for the night on the lee shore of an island. There was a long, shallow stretch of water leading to the land, and so the shore plank would not reach. I stood watching the men slosh through the water to shore, hesitating to submerge my fur-lined boots, when someone shouted, "Hey, Kazan! I think she wants you to *carry* her ashore!"

"Why doesn't she *fly?*" someone else said, and the hooting and laughter started up again. Hot-faced, I clambered over the side of the knarr and splashed through the shallows to land. I stared straight before me, ignoring the men, my ruined boots, and the sopping bottom half of my gown. But out of the corner of my eye I saw Kazan standing still in the water, looking steadily at me. Then someone cuffed him on the shoulder; he laughed, cuffed him back, then went to join his companions.

I stood before the fire to dry myself, nursing my sore, battered limbs and seething in my heart—against these men, against the king and his lady-love, against my father and my mother and my brothers' wives—against all who had conspired to put me in this wretched place.

Still, the smells of cooking tempted me, and when one of the men offered me a bowl of fish stew, a horn of ale, and a hunk of bread, I ate. The bread was fine-grained and white, although stale. The stew had some unfamiliar seasoning in it, but it tasted well enough.

I was tipping back the last of my ale when I heard footsteps beside me. It was the boy—Rath, I'd heard someone call him. In his hands was a screaming, struggling wind gull. I jumped to my feet, enraged that he would treat the poor bird thus, but he blocked my tirade with a torrent of words:

"It was dragging its wing, Lady, I'm sure it's broken or

I would never have picked it up, and you can tell—can't you see?—that it's been starving. And the men, they say you know all about birds, you can call them clear down out of the sky when they're flying, so I thought you might . . . maybe you would know what to do. Because it will die if we leave it here—it can't hunt, something would eat it—and I truly think you should *do* something to save it!"

He stood his ground, this stripling boy in draggled garb, seeming half defiant, half afraid. It was a moment before I recovered my voice. "Let me see it, then," I said.

I took the bird in one hand and spread the other over its back and wings. I could feel its heart pumping fast against my palm; I could sense its panic, a thin cold stream inside my chest. I spoke to it softly, stroking its soft back feathers with my thumb. Its heartbeat calmed. The gull folded its one good wing and calmly looked about.

It was all-over gray—not white on the head and breast as male wind gulls are. A female. She looked thin—too thin. Her keel felt sharp as a knife; she was light as a handful of whiffle fluff. The boy had spoken true: She was starving. Carefully, I stretched out her wounded wing. I ran my fingers lightly along the line of the bone and felt for a break as best I could. I found no break, yet it was hard to be certain. Still, I had had some luck with a bird like this before, simply binding its wings for a time.

"Can you bring me some strips of dry cloth?" I asked the boy. "And a piece of fresh fish?"

Rath scooted away and returned soon with cloth and fish. I tried to recall how I had bound the other bird's wings and, after fumbling a little, folded her two wings close to her body, then contrived to bind them in place by wrapping her about with the cloth. The gull refused to take the fish, so I prized her beak apart and slipped a morsel over her tongue down the back of her throat. When I let go of her beak, she swallowed.

"That will hold her for now, I think," I said, handing Rath the bird.

He turned to go.

"If you like, I can help you feed her in the morning," I said.

"Her? It's a her?"

I nodded.

"I'll bring her, then," the boy said. He turned to go again, and then stopped. "Thank you," he said shyly. He backed off a few steps, then turned and scampered away.

The men had put up a tent, a large one with carved oaken supports, for me alone. Here was royal treatment at last, yet I could not bring myself to be grateful.

I had rather have slept in my bedcloset at home.

I lay in the tent, wrapped in skins, listening to the hiss and rumble of the sea, so unlike the still, friendly lapping of the fjord waters at home. My mind wandered across the unfamiliar new landscape of my life—the journey in the knarr, Rath's wind gull, the young man Kazan, the king's mysterious and frightening summons. What did he want with me? And what was this oath he had made? At last, I let my thoughts touch the hurting places: my mother, my father, my home.

I cried softly, for I wished none of these men to hear.

We were two more days upon the sea. After the first, the waters calmed and the going was neither so wet nor so ache-making as it had been. The snow had stopped, but the wind was incessant and bit deeper as we drew north; no matter how many blankets I wrapped about myself, I never felt warm.

This knarr was full of noise: hearth companions and crew all jumbled in together with horses and cargo—singing, fighting, stomping, cursing, eating. And yet there were moments of quiet, when the cliffs slipped past through the stone-gray sea, and only the creak of a rope, the clap of a wave, the cry of a distant eagle broke the hush.

It was during these times that I worried through my plight. I had tried asking Rog about the king's vow and his plans for me. But the prince had refused to answer, saying only that I would find out soon enough. Rath knew nothing—or claimed to know nothing—and I believed him. Perhaps the king wanted me to call down birds for him—but why I could not fathom. Surely not so that he could shoot them. Surely *he* would not stoop to that.

But something Rog had said at the steading went through and through my mind. *I believe my brother will be of a different mind once he sets eyes upon her. She'll likely be home within a half-moon.*

So I would *be* of no use. Whether I could do what he wanted or no. I would show that I couldn't, or refuse, or pretend not to know how.

And I would be home—home!—within a half-moon.

That first morning before we sailed, Rath fetched me his wind gull to feed. I taught him how to pry open the bird's beak with the fingers of one hand and where to place the fish on her tongue. But soon there was no need to feed by force, for the gull succumbed to her hunger and ate freely from a fist—Rath's or my own.

She began to hop about on the hold; once she jumped onto a barrel and was nearly washed overboard when a wave broadsided the knarr. I devised for Rath a sling carrier of sorts out of a horse's feeding bag. He looked odd, going about his errands with a wind gull poking her head out the top of the bag and glaring at all she saw.

The boy had lost all shyness of me, and, in between running to feed the horses or to fetch bread and ale for the men, he sought me out. We huddled in the lee of barrels and crates, sheltering from the wind, feeling the heave and shudder of the sea-breast beneath us, and he told me of his life. Rath's father, a prosperous steader, had been killed five winters before when Ulian raiders burned his lands. Rath and his mother had escaped to the king's steading, where his mother became a favorite of the king's older sister, Gudjen. But his mother had been taken with the fever and died two years since. As Rath had no other kin, the king's sister had seen to his care. "Some call her a witch," Rath said, "and she is harsh, at times. And strict." He made a face. "She is ever strict. But sometimes I can win my way with her."

I asked him about Kazan, and he told me that the youth was a trader from the land of the Vos.

Of the Vos. I had heard of the Voslanders. They lived east and south of here. Once a trader had come to our steading from that land, bringing honey and spices and vibrant-hued silks. "His ship fetched up on a rock in a storm," Rath continued, "and so he has to winter over with us while it's repaired. The king wants Kazan to build *him* a ship, too—Kazan's is fleeter than any of the king's knarrs, and it handles better, too—but Kazan says that would take overlong. He says it's too cold here. He wants to be trading by spring."

"He seems . . . young to own a ship."

"He's not yet twenty, I think," Rath said. "His father was a trader, too. He's been a ship rat since he was my age— or before."

"Oh," I said. I thought for a moment and then, "Why did he come to fetch *me*?"

Rath shrugged. "Who knows? Kazan . . . has been everywhere. Maybe he hates the idea that there might be one place left in the world that he hasn't yet seen. Or maybe it was birds. Kazan trades in falcons and feathers, along with other things. Maybe he thought that you—"

Falcons and feathers!

Rath broke off, seeing the expression on my face.

What could be more useful than a girl who could call birds down out of the sky so that he could snare them or kill them? I turned away from Rath, trying to hide the rage that choked off my words.

I did not see much more of Kazan—he rode on the other knarr—except that every morning and evening when I waded from shore to knarr or knarr to shore the men stood around joking and hooting and calling out for Kazan to carry me.

I ignored them all.

Still, none of them plagued me otherwise nor caused me to be fearful. I was for the most part left alone.

On the morning of the third day we tacked into a wide bay. The oarsmen furled the sail and began to row. I clambered up into the stem of the ship and faced the breeze, bracing myself against the sea's roll. The bay bent and narrowed until I saw that it was a fjord, a wide-mouthed fjord, hemmed in on either side by rugged cliffs and scaurs that towered skyward. Waterfalls tangled against the rocks like strands of a giant's hair.

Farther on was a place where the cliffs seemed to have

crumbled, and a smooth, rolling valley tumbled to the sea. As we drew near, I saw nestled in the valley the turfed roofs of the largest steading I had ever seen.

"It's the king's steading," said Rath, coming to stand by me. "Or one of them. He has many. But this is northernmost—nearest the dragonlands—and he's been here since the spring."

Dragonlands. My gaze drifted beyond the valley to where white, jagged mountains massed against the sky. This could have nothing to do with that tale they told about me, of when I was small. . . .

No. It could not.

I put away the thought and turned to survey this steading. The wind whipped my hair about my face as Rath pointed out the buildings one by one—so many buildings that I could not without his help have fathomed the uses for them all. There were a high hall, a hearthroom house, a kitchenhouse, a weavinghouse, five courtyard storehouses, and a multitude of byres and sheds and barns. All were made in the way of the buildings on our steading, out of logs and thatched with turf.

Yet unlike in my home, where folk had to wend up a long, steep path from fjord to steading, here the land was so flat that the homefields reached nearly to the wharf. And winter had come earlier here, for snow cloaked the steading and fields.

A cluster of ships lay moored already: another king's knarr with its red, furled sail, and some small fishing boats. A boat shed jutted out over the water.

And now a crowd was gathering. Fishermen left their nets and flocked onto the wharf; women came away from the fish racks to join them. Folk emerged from courtyard and farmyard and field, thronged about by a horde of children and dogs. Rog called out commands to the oarsmen. The knarr glided up to the wharf, and several of the crew jumped out. There was a sudden confusion of shouts and barks and whinnies, a sharp lurch as the ship tilted shoreward, an overwhelming mingled odor of fish and tar and salt.

Rog stepped out and began speaking with a richly garbed woman of about my mother's age.

"There's Gudjen," Rath said. "Here's where I take my leave." He hesitated, then, "Can I come see you tomorrow?" he asked. "Will you look to my bird?"

I nodded. He slipped away through the commotion in the hold and leapt onto the wharf.

Now Rog turned and, motioning for me to come near, held out his hand in courtly wise to help me from the knarr. As if I needed help. He lets me *wade* from knarr to shore these past days, and now he makes a show of gallantry. "Lady Kara," he said, with a slight bow of his head. "Allow me to escort you—"

"Rog, you'll do no such thing," Gudjen said. "Just look at her. What have you *done* with her that she is so bedraggled? Surely she did not set out so; her folk are not of overhigh blood, but they are not—"

I drew myself up, indignant. Gudjen, a tall, hollow-cheeked matron with a beaklike nose, visibly checked herself. "Lady Kara," she said in a somewhat milder tone, "I am Gudjen, sister to the king. You will come with me now and—"

"She will *not* go with you," Rog said. "*I* was sent to fetch her, and fetch her I will, all the way to the king."

"And a poor job you've done of it," Gudjen said. "I gave

you a scarlet cloak to garb her in before you put in to port. Where is it now? Is *that* the one I gave you?" She jabbed a jewel-encrusted finger at the cloak—sodden, dirty, and crumpled behind a cask.

Rog reddened.

"You were to keep it clean and give it to her only when you arrived here. At the very least it would have hidden that, that . . ." Gudjen's eyes said clearer than words what she thought of my best wadmal gown. "And her circlet! What have you done with her circlet! Surely you have not *lost* it!"

"No, I didn't *lose* it," Rog said. "It is only—"

"It's in here," I said, ducking back into the knarr and hurriedly unwrapping the cloak from around the circlet. Gudjen rolled her eyes. I half expected the hearth companions to hoot and jeer at me, but they bustled about their business with eyes averted, suddenly quiet. "She was to wear those *here*," Gudjen said to her brother. "That was why I gave them to you." She sighed. "Come here, come here," she said to me. I stepped back up onto the wharf. "Give them to me." I handed her the circlet and the sodden cloak. Gudjen put the circlet upon my head and thrust the cloak at Rog. "You keep the cloak. It's ruined." She set off down the wharf, motioning me to follow.

Rog grabbed my arm to stop me. *"I am to take her to the king,"* he said. "It is *my* errand."

Gudjen muttered something under her breath, shaking her head. "Rog, Rog, my brother. Think you truly that she is fit to be presented to the king as she now is?"

Rog looked at me a moment and said nothing.

"Think you that *you* are the one to bathe her and dress her and comb her hair?"

Rog swallowed. "I could send a bondmaid to do that, and then—"

Gudjen glanced at me, said a single word: "Come."

I went.

Chapter 3

. . . to see the wide world in a dewdrop's gleam
or glimpse of the morrow in a wisp of steam.

—LINES FROM OLD SPELL

Never had I thought that I would be sorry to leave Rog and his men, but following Gudjen through the folk thronged near the wharf, I devoutly wished I were back on the knarr. The witch, Rath had said some called her. I could well believe it. Gudjen swerved neither right nor left through the crowd but trod straight down the middle of the wharf and up the muddy path to the courtyard, while folk one by one moved aside to let us by. They stared at our faces as we approached, and when I looked back, I saw their still-staring eyes fixed on me.

The king's sister, Gudjen was. I could see that she housewived the steading, for at her waist jangled a golden ring, laden with the household keys. Yet I would have thought

that a king's sister—a princess—would be doing something . . . ladylike. Spinning, perhaps. Or looking to the
larder. Not sparring openly with the leader of the king's hearth
companions—even if he *was* her brother.

At last we reached a small outbuilding at the edge of the
courtyard. The bathhouse, I deemed. Gudjen opened the door;
it was warm inside, and dark. In the light from the smokehole,
I could make out a hearthpit with large, smooth stones ringed
about it. The room seemed like to our bathhouse at home, but
flagstones paved over the dirt floor, and an iron grating spanned
the drain. Smoke twisted up, wafting a breath of burning peat.
To one side of the stones stood a great many urns and pitchers,
each nigh brimful with water.

Gudjen handed me a heap of soft linen. "Put this on,"
she said.

I hesitated.

"Oh, for the love of plunder!" Gudjen turned deliberately
away, muttering in a disgusted tone, "Rustics."

I am *not* a rustic, I thought angrily, as with fumbling
fingers I stripped off my sodden, salt-crusted gown and shift
and leggings. My father holds a steading of seventeen landkir;
I'm not a rustic!

Hastily, I donned the garment she had given me, a short
bath tunic of loosely formed weave. I was accustomed to un-
dressing at bath with my mother and my brothers' wives at
home, but with this witchy, formidable woman I felt . . .
exposed.

Gudjen, absorbed in building up the fire, took no notice
of me. With a long wooden pole she shut the smokehole cover,
a square panel of translucent horn. Dim yellow mist curled
about her; she was a ghostly shadow, haloed in smoke. I heard

the hiss as water struck the hot stones; I recoiled from the sudden explosion of curling steam, which billowed to the rafters.

Around the fire's edge Gudjen trod, pouring water on stone, shrouded in rising plumes of mist. Steam now seethed in the air above our heads. The sound of hissing filled my ears; moisture beaded my face and dampened my hair. I breathed in hard, dragged the hot, heavy air into my lungs until I felt as if they would burst.

The bathhouse blurred, seemed to tip and sway. The floor dipped beneath my feet. In the rafters, churning drifts of mist massed more and more densely together, until I thought—or did I only imagine it? But it seemed as if they were gathering into a shape in the air, something faraway and flying. Flying nearer. Flying fast. There was a rushing noise, the sound of the wind in distant trees as the steam-form took on shape: long and twisting, with wings and a tail, with teeth and glaring eyes.

A dragon shape.

It is not real, I thought. It cannot be real.

And yet it seemed to solidify as I watched, to draw nearer and clearer and brighter, until its back ridge cleaved the darkness, until I kenned the pattern of its scales. It whooshed through the air above me, its breath scorching my face, its wingbeat fanning my hair. I whirled around to watch it as it went, then heard the sigh escape Gudjen's lips: "Ahhhh . . ." And as if blown by the selfsame breath, the dragon began to swirl, to shrink, to thin, to disperse. It rose in tattered clouds, which settled in the rafters until Gudjen opened the smokehole and the bathhouse began to clear. And now my breath came easily, and I could again pick out with my eyes the rafters beneath the thatch, the stones beside the fire, the empty water vessels. . . .

And Gudjen was bringing me a pitcher, telling me to wash and dress, pointing to a heap of clothing on a bench—as if nothing unwonted had passed. "Quickly now," she said. "No time to stand about gaping. I go now to the king; if he is ready, you will be presented to him. When you have dressed yourself, put on these"—here, Gudjen opened a carved oaken box filled with gold and silver jewelry—"*all* of these, mark you? And don't forget the circlet! And comb that hair of yours, too—it's tangled as a crow's nest. Make haste, now, or I will be forced to wash and dress you myself." She paused, and I thought then that she looked at me differently from before. Not with more respect, but with . . . interest.

Then she opened the door and was gone.

I sank down upon the flagstones. My mind felt blurred and numb. That dragon had not been real. Could not have been. It was a vision—only a vision.

Slowly I rose, washed myself with trembling hands, put on the shift and gown she had brought. I felt drained, as if something had been sucked out of me.

The shift, against my skin, felt uncommonly soft. The gown's white wool was thin as silk. About its borders wound strips of tablet weaving, worked in purple and scarlet and gold. Like those on Gudjen's headlinen and gown, I recalled.

As the king's own kin, Rog had said. And now at last it seemed true. But somehow, it made me uneasy. I wanted only to get away from this place. I wanted only to go home.

I fastened the oval shoulder brooches to my gown straps and secured the crimson cape at my throat with the narrow brooch remaining. At last I drew on the boots Gudjen had left for me: supple leather boots the color of fresh-hewn wood.

There was a wealth of rings in the box: arm rings and

neck rings and finger rings; rings of hammered silver and of twisted gold; rings with smooth, smoky stones; rings that glittered with sharply faceted jewels.

Had she said to wear *all* of them? But there were enough finger rings alone for three on every finger. Gudjen herself wore that many but . . . folk would count me overproud to bedeck myself as richly as the king's own sister. I chose a simple twisted neck ring, an arm ring of hammered silver, and a finger ring with a purple stone; the others I left in the box. There was an ivory comb among all the rings; I sat on the bench and tried to settle my mind as I worked the tangles out of my hair.

I must keep my wits about me with the king. I must discover how he wished to make use of me, and then show myself to be of no use. He would find that his efforts were wasted on me—and then he would send me home.

Gudjen soon returned, banged the door shut, strode swiftly across the room, and examined me as if I were a horse to be sold. "I told you to put on the circlet," she said, picking it up and setting it firmly upon my head. "*And* the other rings. Is that too toilsome for you?"

I flushed. "But I will seem . . . overproud."

Gudjen began pulling rings out of the box and jamming them onto my fingers and wrists. "In the king's court we call it not overproud—we call it wealth." She clasped a golden hinged ring about my neck. "If you are to be the king's summoner, you need to look the part."

"But—" I protested.

"At the wharf they saw you dressed in sodden wadmal. Do you want them to deem you a rustic? No." Gudjen answered her own question. "That will not do." She pushed me firmly toward the door.

"Wait," I said, turning to face her. "Rog said I might go home if I . . . if I am of no use to the king."

Gudjen said nothing, but cocked an eyebrow as if to say, *And you believed him?*

"Stand up straight," she said. "Don't slouch! Look neither left nor right, and take no heed of what folk say. Follow me until we come to the hall. Then you must walk alone to the king."

Gudjen strode past me, began to open the door. "Wait!" I said again. "What is this . . . *summoner*, you said. What am I to summon? They promised me this had nothing to do with birds."

"Birds?" Slowly, Gudjen turned around to face me. "Saw you not my steam-working?"

I stared at her, uncomprehending.

"Didn't Rog tell you?"

I shook my head.

Gudjen sighed and pulled the door shut. "Orrik's lady-love, Signy, will not marry him until he slays the dragons that killed her brother and nearly killed her father, the king of Romjek. But of course you must have known *that*."

I gaped. I had known that the king's first wife had died in childbirth, and the long-awaited heir along with her. And Rog had spoken of this lady-love. But slaying dragons . . . that must be the vow he would not explain.

"How do you get by, not knowing the news of the world? No—" Gudjen held up her hand to quell my response. "Don't answer. I don't want to know." She drew in a long breath. "Well. The dragons lair in the mountains north and east of here. They had been preying on the Romjek lambs, as on our own. So Signy's father and her brother and a small warrior band went to clean out the vipers' nest.

"They lost, as I have told you. Now Signy's father lies on his deathbed and cries out to be avenged. He has promised Orrik Signy's hand and rule of Romjek if he succeeds. Then Kragland would be united with Romjek; we would be a force to be reckoned with. Orrik has sworn before all to take up this blood feud, to make Signy's cause his own."

Gudjen paused, and a sick heaviness began to press down upon me, for I knew now where this led.

"They say that you can call down winged things from the sky."

"Birds!" I said. "Only birds!"

"Saw you not my steam-working?" Gudjen repeated. The light from the smokehole fell upon her face and glittered in her eyes.

"You," she said, "will call down dragons for the king."

Chapter 4

For vermilion fever, quaff one full horn dragon's milk
morning and evening, until the eyes turn wholly green.

—KRAGISH FOLK REMEDY

There is a story about me and dragons.

When I had four winters to my life, they say, I was taken with vermilion fever. To this day I have the mark upon my cheek—tiny, needlepricklike scars in the shape of a vermilion blossom. For a half-moon I ate nothing and drank little; my breathing grew fainter and fainter and then stopped.

This is what they tell me. I think of it sometimes, and I wonder if perhaps it was that I did not stop breathing entirely, if perhaps I breathed yet so faintly that they could not mark it. Perhaps they *expected* me to stop breathing, for no one ever before had survived vermilion fever. But when they tell the story, they always say that I had no breath.

They carried me north in a reed-woven casket to a cave

high in the mountains. They held a funeral procession and keening rites, and they strewed me with herbs and dried flowers in the ancient way. Then they went home, left me for dead.

Here there is a gap in the tale, and each teller fills it in his way. My mother says a dragon lived in that cave, and she had lost her young. She breathed her magic breath on me to quicken me to life and nursed me in her draclings' stead.

My father says a baby dragon nipped me and licked the wound to heal it, and my blood began once more to pulse. This dracling, he says, treated me as its own dear sister and brought me bits of food until I grew strong enough to escape.

My aunt once said I was a changeling child—the spirit of a dragon baby breathed into my own dead body and brought back to life. My mother cried when she heard her say it; my father shushed my aunt and commanded her never again to utter that tale.

I remember none of it: nothing of a cave, nothing of dragons. It rankles that each tale treats with dragons, for that part no one saw. True, there were rumors of a dragon hatching in that cave. Many sheep had disappeared from the nearby steadings, and odd, glazed whorls were seen in the snow. My mother says for many moon-turns after I returned, I cried out a dragon name in my sleep.

But who can know for certain what words children cry out in their sleep, or by what names dragons may call themselves?

Still, all agree that a moon-turn after they left me in that cave, I walked whole and hale into a steading, as plump and rosy as if I had never been ill. And yet my cheek was vermilion marked. And another thing: All swear that my eyes were blue before, but since that time they have been green.

As long as I can recall, I have had to live with this dragon tale. I have heard the bondmaids whispering behind my back. I have endured their children calling me "dragon girl." I have seen, from the corners of my eyes, the old crones making the sign against evil as I pass. I have had to listen to my aunt say over and again that no one would marry a girl tainted by dragons; she was as enraged by my two proposals as she was at my turning them down.

And each year the dragons raid more of our sheep at night, and each year the rumblings grow that I am somehow to blame, and each year I escape more and more often into the hills.

I wish they would forget those dragon tales! I hate being the dragon girl!

But my father says the fault is mine that they do not forget. If it weren't for my calling down birds . . .

I remember the day I discovered that not everyone could. I had six winters then, and I called down a raven into the courtyard. I simply held out my arm and called into the sky— aloud, I think—and it grew from a speck to a blotch to a wing-beating, glossy-feathered thing, and it swooped down and lit with a *thunk* upon my wrist. I was admiring the shiny blue-blackness of its eyes when my mother and my aunt and two of my brothers came running, waving their arms and shouting to scare it away. The raven flapped its wings and cawed, but would not release its wiry grip upon my wrist until I turned my eyes away. I felt it push off from my arm, felt the breath of its wingbeat on my face, heard its caw-caw-cawing fade in the distant sky. And there was silence in the courtyard—a silent throng of family and thralls and their children—all staring, stunned, at me.

Perhaps I ought to have quit. I told my father I would. Yet I didn't, and somehow folk knew.

But who would *not* call down birds, once they knew the joy of it?

I see nothing strange in that.

Chapter 5

As the byre cat is kin to the holt cat
and the dog is kin to the wolf
so is the bird kin to the dragon.

—KRAGISH BESTIARY

A throng milled about the door: fishwives and bondmaids, farmers and fishermen and smiths. Gudjen walked directly *into* them as was her wont; folk yielded to her one by one. She looked straight ahead, neither acknowledging their nods nor slackening her pace.

Neither did I look about me, not wanting to meet their frankly staring eyes. I held myself tall and trod carefully in Gudjen's wake, with her words still echoing in my ears:

You will call down dragons for the king.

But I couldn't call down dragons. I'd never *seen* a dragon, unless you credited that tale they told of me. If this was why the king had summoned me, it was all a mistake.

I fastened my gaze on Gudjen's back, trotting, now, to keep up.

I would tell the king that they were wrong about me. I would tell him it was birds I could call—it had nothing to do with dragons. I might even *try* to call a dragon, and prove that I could not.

I clung to the thought as I hastened behind Gudjen through the muddy courtyard, between the turf-roofed storehouses and bakinghouses and weavinghouses. *I will tell the king. He will let me go home.*

A steeply peaked building now loomed before us. The high hall, it must be. Two sentries dragged open the massive wooden doors; there was a cacophony of voices, and winter darkness, softened by drifts of golden light.

"Go," Gudjen said. "I will follow."

I hesitated. My eyes, accustomed to the brightness out of doors, gradually made out the shape of the hall. Narrow, horn-covered windows striped the walls, shedding a dim, honeyed glow across a shifting tide of warriors and an undertow of dogs. A darkish smoke-haze lingered high in the network of beams and rafters, where perched a flock of doves.

One by one the warriors broke off talking and turned to look at me. Silence grew until it seemed to fill the hall, until the doves' placid burbling sounded loud.

I turned round to implore Gudjen to go before me, but again she said, "Go!" and, prodding me forward, whispered, "Curtsy! Do not kneel!"

I walked as I had seen Gudjen do, directly ahead without regard for those who stood in my way, yet sure that no one would yield to me as they had done for her. The nearest man looked square at me and made no move to yield. But just as I slowed my pace to avoid walking into him, he moved the smallest bit and the way before me came clear. Others yielded now, moving little, but enough, until I slowed not at all but strode forward without pause.

Silently, the men yielded, stood before me, yielded. The floor reeds crunched beneath my boots; a whiff of angelica wafted up, mingled with the reeks of sweat and fur and smoke. In the rafters, doves rustled and cooed. The men yielded, stood before me, yielded, until at once the hall was clear and before me I beheld the king.

I knew he must be king. He stood lumined in the shaft of light from the smokehole, set apart from the hearth companions who flanked him on either side. He was clad most richly: in a scarlet cape trimmed with purple-and-gold tablet weaving; in a purple jerkin of soft, napped cloth; in leather boots the color of corberries. His fingers, like Gudjen's, were bedecked with many rings. Upon his head sat a circlet like to mine, but set with a crimson stone.

Curtsy—do not kneel, Gudjen had said.

I curtsied.

"We welcome you, Kara, Asmund's daughter," said the king, striding to greet me. A wolfhound lunged to its feet and sauntered along beside him.

He was tall and lean, this king. I had expected a broader, bearlike man. Faded blond hair curled beneath his helm; his beard, of a darker blond, was streaked with gray. Now he smiled at me, and his face creased like well-worn leather about his mouth and clear blue eyes. I recalled that he was not young. Forty winters, had my father said? Small wonder folk worried themselves about an heir, and rallied round to grant his lady-love's boon.

And yet there was something of the boy about him: a boyish quirk to his smile, a boyish bounce to his gait. He seemed . . . amiable. Far more amiable than his quarrelsome brother and sister.

Tell him, then, I admonished myself. *Tell him you cannot call dragons.*

But the king was asking after my family, and questioning me about my voyage, and querying if there were aught I might need. I answered as briefly as I could, discomfited by the many folk watching.

"And how do your lodgings please you?" he asked.

"She has not"—Gudjen's voice came from just behind me—"has not yet seen her lodgings, my brother, for I would not take her to them. Rog"—Gudjen's voice dripped with scorn—"has taken it upon himself to remove her belongings to the bursloft with the serving women."

"They are freeborn maids and not thralls!" Rog stepped forward from the band of hearth companions. "I see no reason why she should not—"

Gudjen did not deign to address Rog but spoke directly to the king. "She is the daughter of a loyal and prosperous subject, my brother, a steader of seventeen landkir. And so I have sent word that her belongings be removed to the royal women's quarters—"

"The royal women's quarters!" Rog exploded. "Our sister forgets that *I* fetched this girl from her home and saw what she is accustomed to. The bursloft will be luxury for her!"

I felt my face grow hot. "Hush you!" the king said in a low, angry voice. "This talk is unseemly here and now. Speak to me later, alone."

"Orrik." Gudjen's voice was soft but intense. "What this girl can do with birds has been witnessed by many. And well you know what is said of birds and dragons. They are akin: What one hears, the other hears also; what one obeys, so obeys the other. Yet none but I know what I worked in the steam of her: a dragon that came at her behest."

The king gripped his sister's arm. "Are you certain? At her behest?"

Gudjen nodded. "She is what you have sought all this time; she will succeed where *others'* ploys have failed." She fixed Rog with a meaningful stare.

"I didn't fail!" Rog sputtered. "Never say that I failed!"

Gudjen ignored him. "Her fate is tied to yours in this matter. She . . ." Gudjen went on, and I saw the king was attending her, seemingly torn between stifling the row and hearing what she had to say.

Why did she press so hard? I wondered. To thwart Rog only? Or for some other cause?

"Nothing is proven of her, save for a passel of old wives' tales from those bumpkins at her steading!" Rog's voice was low, but his face crimsoned with reined-in rage. "I tell you, she cannot call down a dragonfly, never mind a dragon. And just see how she dresses! She wears more gold than my wife. More than our own mother! It is unseemly in one born to her state. And see how she did not deign to nod as folk yielded to her but kept her nose in the air, as if she were royalty itself. Neither did she kneel before you, my brother, but only curtsied. She is arrogant! A crude, grasping country girl of paltry means and no power—"

"Cease this! Both of you!" King Orrik roared. In the abrupt silence he sighed and then shook his head. "Must you two bicker over everything? Must you nip and yap at me like ill-trained pups?"

But I no longer listened. *Lowborn! Grasping! Unseemly!* I felt emptied of breath, as if someone had clouted me in the stomach.

"My brother, one small token of proof!" Rog insisted. "You demean yourself and all our family to house this wench in the royal chambers! Likely she will take up all the gold she can lay hands on and abscond with it. All I ask—all *we* ask—" he raised his voice to an oratorical pitch and gestured at the folk in the hall—"is one small proof. One dove, called down from the rafters. Surely that is little enough to ask!"

The throng in the hall began to murmur; someone shouted out, "Proof!" The king looked out at them, then back at me. His blue eyes wavered for a moment, then he shrugged as if in apology. "Lady Kara, if you would . . . one dove." He held out both hands in a flourish, as if presenting me to them.

Lowborn. Crude. Arrogant. Will take up all the gold she can lay hands on and abscond with it.

For one fleeting moment I minded me of my resolve to prove I could do nothing; then the moment was gone. I glared at Rog, anger scalding my veins. *I never asked for this. You took me from home against my will, and now you revile me. No power? We shall see.*

I looked up toward the rafters, where the doves still burbled and cooed. I held out both arms and called, loud as thunder in my mind.

There was a trembling, a ripple of light, as first one dove, then another and another stirred upon its perch. Then a surge, a stream of pulsing movement, until the air throbbed with beating wings: wings from the doves in the rafters, a noisy torrent of wings pouring in through the smokehole from the sky. The whole upper portion of the war hall seemed to lift and wheel and cascade down to me. Doves alit upon my arms, my shoulders, my hair. They hooked their sharp claws into my cloak and gown until I was draped with them—head and shoulders and halfway to the floor—a heavy white mantle of cooing, fluttering doves.

The throng had fallen silent; the king stared; Rog gaped. I thought I saw Gudjen smile and then quickly suppress it.

But she could not hide the triumph in her eyes.

Chapter 6

*Second only to the eagle in nobility and fierceness
is the gyrfalcon.*

—THE FALCONER'S ART

"Kara!"

I opened my eyes and looked about me but could
see little in the gloom of my bedcloset. Had someone whispered
my name?

I sat up beneath the bedclothes—two goosedown bolsters
and three feather-stuffed quilts, with a thick sheepskin covering over all. Even the mattress was filled with feathers rather
than straw—luxury unheard of in my home. I opened my
bedcurtains the tiniest crack. In the ruddy glow of the braziers
I could see draperied beds all arow along the wall. At the
end was the king's mother's enormous bed, around which her
bondmaids slept on pallets on the floor.

Nothing stirred.

"Kara!" came a voice from the other side of my bed. "It's

42

me, Rath. Would you wake up! They'll catch me if you don't, and—"

Rath!

I wrapped myself in sheepskin, flung open the drape, and looked out—into the eyes of the strangest-looking creature I had ever beheld. It wore a matron's headlinen, but tilted all askew. The sleeves of its gown hung down below its hands; its shawl dragged on the floor. It grinned impishly. . . .

"Rath!"

"Kara," he whispered urgently, "I had to see you, but they wouldn't let me. They won't let anybody near you anymore. They won't even *tell* you something for me. Listen, can you come to the mews today? My wind gull's there and she's faring well enough, but I want *you* to see her. The falconer says she's well and it's not time to take off her bindings, but . . . can you come? He has other birds I deem you'd like. I told him all about you, and he's heard about the doves— everybody's heard about that—but I don't think he *understands* about you and . . . can you come? *Can* you?"

As before, it took a moment to recover myself from Rath's torrent of words. "I—I don't know if Gudjen will brook it," I said, keeping my voice low. "Where is the mews?"

"Behind the old smithy, past the cow shed. Will you come?"

"I don't know, I—"

"You little whelp!" Gudjen bore down upon him from around the bedcurtain. Rath fluttered his arms and babbled in a high, womanish voice, meanwhile bolting for the door. Quick as an eel, Gudjen snatched off his headlinen and latched onto his ear. Twisting it, she held him fast. "Don't you ever let me find you here again. Do you mark me?"

Rath seemed to want to nod but couldn't move his head.

"You're wearing out my patience with your tricks. There was that frog—the one that leapt into the queen mother's lap at supper—"

"But it was *wounded*," Rath said. "I only set it on the table for a moment."

"Heed yourself," Gudjen said, twisting his ear harder. "Do you hear me?"

"Yes, Lady!" Rath gritted his teeth against the pain; his face was turning red.

"Now, go." Gudjen released Rath's ear and gave him a shove toward the door. "And don't come plaguing the Lady Kara again."

She looked after him as he left, shaking her head, and a fond smile crossed her lips, as if she couldn't suppress it.

"He was on the ship with me," I said. "I set a bird's broken wing for him, and he wants me to look to it now."

"You are not to do what eight-winters-old boys want you to do," Gudjen said. "You are to do what the king wants you to do."

"But I can't do what *he* wants me to do," I said. "I have told and told you this. I can't call dragons—only birds."

"We will see," Gudjen said. She turned toward her mother's bed and disappeared behind the curtains.

Slowly, I began to dress. Oh, *why* had I lost my temper and called down those doves? That had been three days ago, and now I was a prisoner. A cosseted prisoner, surely—I had a handmaiden and fine gowns, and all called me Lady Kara. Indeed, they did treat me well—with respect—which was far different from the way things stood at home. Yet Gudjen kept me pent up with the king's mother's women all the day long. I was not allowed even to *see* another soul except during meals.

And the king was planning something, a journey, I had heard. But no one would speak of it to me. I knew only what I overheard: talk of warriors coming from afar, of weapons, of charts, of mountains to the east. Talk of me . . .

You will call down dragons for the king, Gudjen had said. And now, because of the doves, they all believed it. Yet here, *dragon girl* seemed not the curse it was at home. There folk deemed me in league with dragons. Here I was allied in a great and popular cause against them.

Now I heard the chink of Gudjen's keys and footfalls moving toward the door. I leapt from my bed and ran to stop her. "Rath," I said, "wants me to visit the mews, and I would like to do this. Surely there could be no harm—"

"No telling where harm may lie," Gudjen said shortly. "A maid of your station does not go flitting about the steading like a scullery girl. The king has taken you as his ward; your conduct reflects on him. Besides, the king has enemies. *You* may have enemies. In any case, the queen mother expects you for tablet weaving today."

Tablet weaving again! This was worse, if possible, than spinning. My mother owned one gown with a tablet-woven strip on it, which she had had all her grown life. No one had leisure for tablet weaving on our steading. It was enough to card and spin and weave the plain wadmal cloth we needed.

All these past two days I had spent in the weavinghouse, grappling with the strange bone plaques with holes in them, poking my fingers with needles, unraveling threads from the tangled mats I made of them. Tablet weaving! And through it all the queen mother complained—of gout, of colic, of pains in her fingers and aches in her back. Rog's meek, pallid wife fussed over her and sent bondmaids hastening to and from the herbary with medicinal draughts and balms.

45

Gudjen, I marked, had not lingered in the weavinghouse these past two days but had hastened straight away, "to attend to household matters," she said. Had I not been kept like a caged bird, I would have devised matters to attend to as well.

Now, as if kenning my thoughts, Gudjen said, "Enjoy this snug harbor while you may, child. For the king is plotting a dragon hunt. The day will soon come when you long for the safety and comfort of women's work." She turned on her heel and was gone.

Yet on this morning the fates were with me. I broke my fast in the high hall, hedged about by the queen mother's women at the high table. The king was much preoccupied with Kazan this day; I kept my gaze fixed on my trencher, for I did not wish to speak with Kazan, or even attract his notice.

All at once I heard cries from without, and a housecarl burst in, babbling of something—I could not understand what. The folk nearest him rose from their benches and ran from the hall. "Fire," I heard as they fled, and "kitchenhouse," and "water." Alarm spread through the hall in ripples, circling out from where the housecarl had come in. Someone, it seemed, had dropped a lighted faggot on the kitchenhouse floor, and the rushes had caught fire, and the whole building was imperiled. A chaos of shouts and scraping benches and jostling bodies enveloped me as wave upon wave of diners surged for the door.

I stepped outside and watched as folk carrying all manner of ewers and barrels and buckets converged upon the smoking kitchenhouse. More folk thronged about the well, waiting for water; still more streamed into the courtyard from the barnyard and fields. Soon, I thought, they would have this fire well in hand. They had no need of me.

All at once, I was seized by the urge to escape.

But where to?

The mews, Rath had said. Behind the old smithy, past the cow shed.

I slipped through the crowd, picking my way through the churning mud. Snow was falling lightly, flurried about by the wind. I lingered at the stables, now strangely deserted. Stroking a big bay's muzzle, I breathed in the familiar smells of hay and horseflesh and manure. I passed by the byre with its chickens and goats. The flock was still on the hillside; I judged it would not be brought to byre until winter hardened its grip. I peeked into the cow shed and into the dairy hard beside.

At last I found the mews, behind the old smithy as Rath had said. It was a long stone building with horn-covered windows overlaid by vertical slats of wood.

The door stood closed. I tugged at the latch; it opened. I peered in. "Hello?" I said.

No reply.

I stepped within. Despite the windows, it was much darker here than without, and at first I could not see well at all. A dusty smell tickled my nose—of sawdust, of mingled herbs, of leather and smoke and feathers. I heard a tinkling of bells and the dry *click click click* of talons stepping across a perch.

Slowly the shapes came clear. I made out a cauldron above a still-smoking firepit, and several three-legged stools. One had been knocked over onto its side; a welter of leather strips and a half-eaten wedge of bread lay in the sawdust beside it, as if someone had left in haste. And something else: a soft lump of clay, shaped vaguely like a bird.

Against one wall stood a rough wooden bench, strewn

about with all manner of small knives and odd-looking instruments, as well as scraps of sacking and leather and cord.

I drew near the bench. Above it, tiny bells and interlinked metal rings hung from a row of nails. And above these, lined upon a shelf, were the most wonderful things of all: tiny, exquisitely wrought hoods, each topped by a tiny black plume.

There was a chirruping noise, the sound that hawks make deep in their throats. I looked far down the length of the room. There, on a row of perches, with the morning sun laying bars of golden light across them, were birds. Big birds: hunting birds.

Slowly, I drew near. There was a goshawk, I saw, and a mountain falcon. A hunchbacked hawk and . . . was that a red-winged falcon? The wings were only tipped with red, but it might be a redwing in its youthful plumage. At the end of the row, screened off from the other birds by a stack of wooden boxes, perched a tiny kestrel. They all stood tense and alert, as if *listening* to see what I would do next.

For a moment I forgot to breathe, they were so wild, so magnificent.

<Hello,> I said, inside my mind. <Hello.>

They regarded me for a long, slow heartbeat of time. Then the redwing rattled its feathers, and the mountain falcon scratched its chin with a talon, jingling its bells. The goshawk turned its back to me, and the kestrel did a cross-step dance across its perch.

So. I was accepted. Or tolerated, at least.

Each bird had its own perch, a flat wooden bar below which hung a length of canvas. Fastened to each perch was a leather leash, which in turn was tied to the thin leather jesses that encircled the birds' legs.

48

So these were screen perches. I had heard tell of them from a falconer who once came to our steading. The canvas gave the birds a way to climb back up to their perches when they bated. Without it, they could hang themselves.

Where was Rath's wind gull? I cast about me and at once caught sight of an odd-looking wooden box. There she was—the wind gull, sitting upon a perch set low inside the box. Her wings were still bound with the cloth I'd used. "Hello, old friend," I said. She cocked her gray head and gave a hoarse peep.

I was checking her bindings when I heard a rustling from an unexpected quarter—the dark far end of the mews. I turned and looked, then walked slowly toward what I had thought must be a storeroom.

It was not a storeroom. It was a mew of thin wooden slats that ran from floor to thatch. There was a door, large enough for a man to enter, standing. And something within, something ghostly white. A snowy owl, perhaps?

Drawing closer, I discerned its shape—not an owl's shape. It was . . . I peered between the slats. It was a gyrfalcon, an arctic gyrfalcon. I had seen gyrfalcons before, of course, cavorting in the wind streams above our steading. But none so white as this. It must hie from the far, far north, where the whitest gyrfalcons dwell. Its fierce black eyes glared at me. It tugged at my heart. So wild, so beautiful to be imprisoned in this gloomy cage . . .

I slipped the bolt from its hasp and opened the mew door. The falcon sidestepped on its perch, bobbing its head. I closed the door behind me and wrapped a piece of my cape about my fist. This bird was unjessed, I saw.

<Come,> I summoned silently, and felt a tremolo of

resistance in my mind: a pulling-away, a walling-off from me. Falcons do that; it's seldom they will come for me, save for the little merlins and kestrels.

<Come.>

The bird lowered its head and twisted sideways, watching me closely out of a malevolent eye.

Surely it wouldn't . . . attack.

I swept the fear from my mind. <Come.> Slowly, I raised my fist. <Come.>

I felt something, then: a softening, a guttering away of rage. Then something else. A greeting? No, liker to . . . recognition.

The falcon pushed off its perch, swooped, thumped down, and clutched my fist. It was heavy; its big, powerful talons pierced the cloth. I flinched but held myself still. It stared at me; I averted my eyes, as is polite with birds. Yet still I felt it: a rippling in my mind, stronger than ever I had known.

I spoke to it soothingly, afraid, just yet, to stroke it. I turned—slowly, carefully—until the bird was touched with light. It was not completely white, I saw. Black arrow-shaped markings flecked its head and wings. Its thighs were clothed in pale yellow down, all the way to its feet. They looked for all the world like baggy leggings. Its feet and cere were pale yellow, its beak bluish gray, like slate.

I could not tell by its coloring whether it were male or female, but it was big—nearly as long as my forearm—so I guessed it must be female.

"You're beautiful," I said. "Do you know that?"

The gyr fluffed its feathers—*her* feathers, I corrected myself. She looked at me as if I had said something ridiculously obvious.

I was just reaching slowly to stroke her when the outer

door creaked open. The bird pulled up straight, eyes alert, feathers closed tight. In walked a stranger, flanked by Rath and a very young girl. They were talking as they came, not seeing me. Then at once the man drew up short. He motioned Rath and the girl to stay back. Slowly he moved toward me, right to the gyrfalcon's mew, and eyed me between the slats.

"Get out," he said in a voice ominously soft, "before I choke you with my own bare hands."

Chapter 7

At the world's edge lies a land called Thrym
where steam seeps from the skin of the earth
and snow-bearded peaks breathe fire.

—KRAGISH SEAFARERS' LORE

I stepped back, startled. The gyrfalcon screamed, tightened her grip on my hand. One wing clouted my head, and then the bird was flying. She crashed into the slatted door and tumbled to the ground in a flurry of feathers.

"Get out *now*," the man said.

"She may be hurt!" I bent down to look, fearful for the bird.

"Now. Out!" The door opened behind me; the man reached in, grabbed my arm, and roughly dragged me back. The bird's harsh keening tore at my heart. She launched herself into the air. I staggered backward past the door; the man slammed it shut just as the bird hit the slats.

She fell again, still screaming.

"If you've hurt her, if you've ruined her for hunting I'll—

I'll ruin *you*," the man said through clenched teeth, pulling me back and away from the mew.

"*I* ruin her!" I protested. "She was well before you came."

"No one is permitted within that mew. No one is permitted *near* that mew, except for me. Do you ken me? I have spent a half-moon gentling her, and you may have undone it all. She cost the king a fortune. She is worth . . ." He glanced at the bird, hunkered on the ground, and his eyes softened.

"Corwyn?" Rath was tugging at the man's tunic, but he didn't seem to notice. "Corwyn!" Rath said again. The little girl peered out from behind him, her dark eyes trained on me.

"She is worth five fortunes," the man murmured, as if to himself.

He was a big man, stout of girth, though not, I saw, so tall as first I had thought him. His face was clean-shaven. His hair, reduced on top to a few thin strands, was a deep shade of brown. Corwyn, Rath had called him. An Elythian name. But . . . wasn't the queen mother's healer an Elythian named Corwyn?

Now he turned and glowered at me. "I want you out of here—now. You could have caused her to break her wings. You may yet have done so."

I was stung by the unfairness of this. "*I* did not harm her. She flew to my fist. She was settled there, serene as a suckling lamb. Then you frightened me, and that frightened her."

"She *flew* to your fist? She flies to no one's fist—not even mine. You must have enticed her with meat, although how—" He stopped, his eyes narrowing, taking in my gown, my rings, my circlet. "Who are you?" he asked. "Your face is not known to me."

"I've been trying to tell you, Corwyn! This is Kara." Rath waved at me. "Hullo, Kara. You're bleeding."

53

I looked down at my wrist. Blood welled out from where the gyrfalcon's talons had pierced through the cloth to my skin. I hadn't marked it before, but now that I had, it hurt. I should have known better than to call a falcon, gloveless.

"Kara?" the man was saying. "This is the one you told me of? The king's dragon girl? Gudjen's ward?"

"Yes," Rath said. "She's good with birds. I told you so. And the gyr *was* preening herself on Kara's fist when we came in. I saw. And look now. She's back on her perch, and not a sign of harm about her."

The little girl poked her head out from behind Rath. Catching my glance, she dived behind him again.

Corwyn was studying the bird. She had stopped screaming but still shuffled from side to side on her perch, bobbing her head and warily eyeing us. He turned back, regarded me appraisingly. His shrewd, intelligent eyes seemed to encompass all of me at once.

"So," he said at last. And then gruffly, "I had best make a poultice for that wrist of yours. If it festers, Gudjen will have me flayed."

In a nook behind the door stood a small workbench, which I had not seen when I came in. Atop it were two narrow shelves, crammed with all manner of jars and bottles, flagons and vials. Herbs hung in bunches from the ceiling; three brass scales and an assortment of stone bowls were arrayed upon the bench.

An herbary? I was confused. "Are you . . . the healer?" I asked.

Corwyn nodded curtly, motioning me to the bench. He unstoppered a vial containing a strange blue liquid; its acrid smell overwhelmed the herbs' delicate pungence. Rath and the little girl looked on as Corwyn poured the liquid onto my arm.

It stung.

"Ouch!" I said, pulling away.

"Corwyn is the king's own mother's healer," Rath said as Corwyn set to mixing various sharp-smelling liquids and powders in a small stone bowl. "The king sent for him all the way from Elythia to attend Prince Rog when his arm was festering. Corwyn cured it, and now the queen mother won't let him go. She needs him for *her* ailments—"

"Fanciful ailments," Corwyn muttered under his breath.

"But I thought he—you," I amended, turning to Corwyn. "I thought you were the king's falconer."

He slathered my wrist with a cool green paste before answering. "I learned much of herb lore in tending to birds. It was but a short jump to tending folk."

"Now folk come to him from everywhere," Rath said. "He's the best healer for three kingdoms round. The best falconer, too."

Corwyn made a gruff shushing noise. He began to wind my wrist about with strips of linen cloth. The cuts had stopped hurting without my being aware of it; the poultice still felt cool.

The little girl—of four or five winters, I guessed—had picked up the clay from the floor and was working it in her hands. Her hair and eyes were dark, like Corwyn's.

"And who are you?" I asked her. She scrambled behind Corwyn.

"My daughter, Myrra," Corwyn said. "Myrra, come out. It's nothing to fear."

Myrra sidestepped out into view, looking tiny beside the

broad bulk of her father. She quickly ducked her head—but not before I caught a flash of smile.

Now Corwyn fastened the linen strips with a neat knot. "So," he said, turning my wrist in his hands to inspect his work. "You can call down birds from the sky, or so they say. Could you call, say, Gussie—that goshawk—from her perch?"

I surveyed the hawk. Her red-gold eyes, slightly flattened on top, gave her a wild, intent expression. Her beak was cruelly hooked; her talons, huge. She was big—bigger than any bird I'd called before, save for the gyrfalcon.

Gussie fixed me with her red-gold glare; I sensed her seeking me.

"I . . . think I can call her," I said.

"Shall we put it to the proof?"

I shrugged. "Very well."

Hanging from the edge of the workbench were a passel of left-handed leather gloves, gauntleted to the elbow. Corwyn unhooked one and handed it to me. I slipped it onto my hand, and he did the same with another.

Corwyn loosed the goshawk's jesses from her leash and, speaking to her softly, touched the back of her legs. The bird stepped backward onto his gauntlet.

"Stand by the door," he said, "and call."

<Come.> I directed my thoughts to Gussie. <Come.>

I felt the rippling of hawk consciousness in my mind as the bird bobbed her head, then hunched her wings and crouched down on Corwyn's wrist.

<Come.>

She leaned forward, unfolded her mottled brown wings, and then she was airborne, pumping through the sun-streaked gloom of the mews. A breath of air on my cheek, a thump on my wrist; the bird clumsily alit, flapped, nearly fell off, then at the last moment regained her balance. I teased her breast feathers upward, murmuring soft praise. She drew up and stretched out her wings, pleased with herself.

Rath was smiling broadly. "Good girl, Gussie," he said, pantomiming applause.

Myrra, aping Rath, did the same. "Good Gussie, good Gussie."

Corwyn favored me with that level, appraising look again. He reached behind him; when he held up his hand there was a dead mouse between his gloved fingers. He whistled.

I let my mind go away from the hawk; she pushed off from me and flew to Corwyn's fist. When she had done gobbling the mouse, Corwyn set her on her perch and retied the jesses.

"What you do does not seem so different from what I do," I said.

"Save for that you do it without bait, without training, and without familiarity with the bird," Corwyn replied, "which makes it very different, indeed."

We flew the kestrel and the hunchback and the redwing in the same wise, with me summoning them off Corwyn's fist, and Corwyn whistling them back for food. Corwyn mellowed as we worked, although he still eyed me from to time as if he did not know what to make of me. As I watched him now, he seemed not so harsh as I had thought him before. Truly he seemed not harsh at all, but only tender for the care of his birds. He and Rath and Myrra told me the names of the birds, and their histories, and the quirks of their various tempers.

The goshawk, Gussie, had been taken as an eyas from her nest and had virtually to be taught how to fly. "That's why she's so clumsy," Rath said.

"She's a clodhopper!" Myrra put in.

"She hunts middling well," Corwyn said, "but she'll never equal a passager or a haggard."

"That means captured on its first migration," Rath said. "I mean, passager does. And haggard is a bird that's captured when it's older."

The red-winged falcon was named Erik, after a warrior Corwyn knew. He was of stippled grays and browns, with red-tipped wings that, Corwyn said, would turn entirely red at his next molt. A thin, feathered mustache ran along the top of his beak and partway down his neck.

"And that hunchbacked hawk is Slouch," Rath said. I smiled, for Slouch's black-capped head jutted forward, making his shoulders look hunched.

"Don't forget Killer!" Myrra piped up.

"The kestrel," Rath said.

I laughed. Such a fierce name for so tiny a thing. She was striking, with her blue-black eyes, creamy black-flecked breast, and foxy-brown wings. And that she *was* a terror to mice I had no doubt.

The mountain falcon, Bruta, was an ill-tempered gray-and-white haggard whom none but Corwyn could fly. "Best hunter of the lot, and she won't tolerate the king," Corwyn said. "And Rog even less. She footed him badly some years ago—caused the nasty abscess I was summoned to cure. He's never so much as approached a hunting bird since."

"After Corwyn's done training the gyr, only the king will hunt her," Rath said.

"But perhaps you might try Bruta one day when you are better known to her," Corwyn offered.

I nodded—a false nod—for at once I minded me of Gudjen, and the king's mother's ladies, and tablet weaving.

My heart sank. I would never become better known to Bruta nor any of the other birds. Gudjen would not deem it fitting for me to loiter about the mews. She would never permit me to come here again.

I did not ask to fly the gyrfalcon, and Corwyn did not offer so much as to let me approach her mew. But she had taken hold of my thoughts, that fierce, splendid white one. I recalled her wild blue-black eye and the pulse of recognition that had rippled through my mind. And a longing grew inside me to see her, to call her, to hold her again upon my fist.

We were admiring Rath's wind gull, which he had named Hild, when the outer door opened and someone came in. Kazan, the trader. I felt myself stiffen. He paused a moment, then strode forward.

"So, Kazan!" Corwyn said, moving to meet him. "What brings you here? If you've come to see me fly that falcon of yours, you're early, by a moon-turn, at least."

Kazan smiled and shook his head. "No, I come . . . for Kara," he said in his odd, clipped speech. He leaned around Corwyn to address me. "Gudjen is—" He hesitated, seeming to seek the right word. "Displeased," he said at last. "She has gone floor-reeds to roof-turf searching for you."

Displeased? She was furious, like as not.

"I thought . . . you might be here," Kazan said. He waited, his gaze steady but not overbold. He did not say why *he* had come to fetch me.

I sighed, feeling my freedom slipping away from me.

"You're not taking her back, are you?" Rath asked. "Kara can make the hawks fly to her. You can watch, too."

"I would like to see that one day," Kazan said.

One day when you have your snares with you, I thought bitterly.

59

"But Gudjen wants you now, and . . ." Kazan shrugged.

And what Gudjen wants, Gudjen gets, I thought.

"But Kazan," Rath persisted, "could you not go back and tell Gudjen you have found Kara and she is safe? Could you not leave her here a little while yet?"

"Let her stay! Let her stay!" Myrra chimed in.

Kazan still said nothing, but gazed steadily at me.

"Corwyn?" Rath said. "Tell him she can stay! It's well with you, is it not?"

To my surprise, Corwyn seemed regretful. "For me it is well. But Gudjen wants her and . . ."

And what Gudjen wants, Gudjen gets.

I took a long, last look back at the mews, at Rath and Corwyn and Myrra, and the birds I had just begun to know. I turned toward the gyrfalcon's mew, and I marked a light, fluttering form behind the slats.

"Lady Kara?" Kazan said, motioning me to the door. He crooked his elbow, inviting me to take it. Startled, I looked up and found myself staring straight into his long dark eyes, nearly on a level with my own. I broke away, strode past him into the barnyard.

"I am going," I said.

In silence, we walked toward the courtyard.

I had not meant to speak to Kazan on our way back. But something Corwyn had said snagged in my mind, and at last I had to ask. "Corwyn said . . . *your* falcon. Which one is yours?"

Kazan smiled. "I have no falcon. But Corwyn calls the gyr mine, for it was I who snared her and brought her to your king."

"You?" At once I felt foolish. Of course it had been Kazan. The falcon was newly come here. And Kazan traded in falcons—I knew that well enough.

My surprise must have shown, for Kazan laughed and said, "Did you think I would not sail so far north, despising *this* as I do?" He held up his hands to the snow, which whirled about more thickly than before. "But . . . I must go where there are goods to trade, like it or no. And even when I am lost, I find *something*."

"Lost?" I had not meant to encourage him, but my curiosity was caught.

As we walked up through the barnyard, Kazan told me of a storm at sea that drove his ship north—farther north than ever he had been. He had thought that he and his crew would die in the open sea, so far had they strayed from the known lands—until they sighted the cliffs through the fog. There they found birds and foxes and walruses and whales and other creatures far more plentiful than ever they had seen. And not a sign of man, or that man had ever trod this land before.

"But most strange were these . . . smokes that went up from the land. Not fire-smokes. Water-smokes. We found a place where water bubbled up from a cleft in the rock—so hot, it boiled our meat. The ground where we slept felt warm, as if a fire burned beneath it. And inland there were ice-bound mountains that breathed out steam.

"We set out our traps and snares; there was wealth enough in that place to fill our hold many times over. Yet on the second day one of the mountains cleared its throat and began to spit fire and ash into the air. And the sky turned black as a moonless, starless night."

They had set sail at once. There was time only to take up a few snared birds, the white gyr among them.

I had nearly forgotten about Gudjen, so taken was I with this tale of Kazan's. But now I saw her tacking toward us through the whirling snow, brisk as a ship under a stiff breeze.

Kazan turned to me, intent. "I wish you could have seen that place," he said. "You could have called a *thousand* birds, they were so thick."

I recoiled as if I had been slapped. So this was what he was leading to. A thousand white falcons would make him wealthier than the king!

I turned abruptly from Kazan and hastened for Gudjen and the tongue-lashing she had in store.

A nd yet someone must have spoken to Gudjen later that day, for in the evening before we supped she took me aside and said that I might spend my days in the mews with Corwyn, instead of with the queen mother's women. I gaped at these tidings, for they went entirely at odds with the harsh words she had had for me earlier, when I had returned from the mews.

Now she grew stern all at once and said that I must do as Corwyn bade me, that it was cold and damp and dirty in the mews, but that I had better not complain after all the vexation I had caused her. Hastily I agreed, before she could change her mind.

And then a further astonishment: On my way to the women's quarters after supper, Corwyn appeared at my side. "You come to the mews on the morrow?" he asked.

"Yes," I said. "Do I have you to thank for this? It is . . . beyond what I dared hope."

Corwyn brushed aside my thanks. "Come at early morn, and we will begin work with the gyrfalcon."

"The gyrfalcon! But you said—"

"All is now changed. The king has given the gyrfalcon to you. *Given* her. You had best thank him first chance, for it is a great honor—greater, I think, than you know. Since his last gyr died he has not had a falcon proper to his rank. But Orrik has his purposes, and now the bird is yours."

For the second time that night I stood gaping. "Remember—early morn," Corwyn said. He turned on his heel and strode away.

The gyrfalcon was *mine*. And Corwyn would train me to fly her. This was a thing of such wonderment, I could barely credit it. To fly the gyrfalcon . . . *Mine.*

I should have been overjoyed, and yet . . . a wisp of unease trailed through my mind. It was so sudden, so much of a change. What had brought this about?

Orrik has his purposes, Corwyn had said. And now I minded me of what Gudjen had said of birds and dragons: *They are akin: What one hears the other hears also; what one obeys, so obeys the other.*

And I knew it as strongly as I knew my own name: This kindly, amiable king was using me, was using the gyr, was using us both to achieve his own end.

Chapter 8

*When you see wax on her claws and beak, you
will know she has silera. Here is the cure: Take
a black snake and fry it in a pan. Mix the cooked
fat with peppercorns and grouse flesh and feed this
to the falcon for nine days.*

—THE FALCONER'S ART

The mews was dark when I arrived, save for a haze of golden lamplight that pricked the surfaces of Corwyn's apothecary vials and illuminated his hands.

I hesitated a moment, watching those hands, large and bluntly shaped yet deft of movement, gloved in tattered linen with the fingers cut away. Corwyn turned, nodded to me, then resumed his work: decanting a sharp-smelling purple liquid into a paste of musky herbs.

"For bumblefoot," he said. "Bruta suffers from it; daily we must make the salve."

The hearthfire dwindled low; Corwyn instructed me to stoke it. I found the bellows and pumped the smoldering coals to a rosy glow, then put on a split log from the woodpile under the eaves. The blaze crackled to life, sending out waves of gratifying warmth.

I stole a look down the length of the mews, where the hawks drowsed on their perches. The far end, where the gyrfalcon was mewed, lay deep in shadow. But I thought I saw a dim, blurry whiteness go streaking across the dark. My heart stirred. *She was mine.* I could scarce believe it.

"Draw water from the well and fetch it here," Corwyn said, "for we have much to do."

I did as he bade me. Next, he had me fill a cart with fresh sawdust. I had thought to begin work with the gyrfalcon forthwith and began to feel impatient of these chores. Yet Corwyn spoke no word of the gyr. Instead, he summoned me to watch as he took up Gussie from her perch and carried her to his bench. Gussie stretched up and looked about. Her red-gold gaze met mine; she held still for a moment, then roused and began to preen.

Corwyn ran his fingers through Gussie's feathers—seeking out mites, he told me—and checked her eyes for running matter. He lifted each talon, explaining why he did so all the while. The bumblefoot, he said, causes a bird's foot to swell and redden. It is best to find it when it starts and treat it then.

Then he set Gussie on a brass scale and wrote her weight on a marked-up sheet of parchment. "For if she grows too fat, she will not fly for quarry," he said, "but neither should she be too thin."

At last he slipped a small plumed hood over her head, securing it with a leather thong.

"Why did you hood her?" I asked.

"Often I hood them during the day, to close out distractions and keep them calm."

Corwyn taught me to check the sawdust beneath the hawks' perches for signs of disease in their castings and mutes. He told me to sweep away the old sawdust and strew the floor with new as each bird was removed from its perch. At this, I felt the stirrings of rebellion inside me. When would we work with the gyr? But Corwyn, perhaps guessing my thoughts, said, "This checking is crucial work. I have always done it myself, but I think I may now entrust it to you."

Then Corwyn attended to each and every bird. I bit my tongue and bided until we would work with the gyr. From time to time Corwyn called me to watch him: straightening this bird's twisted feathers with hot water, coping that one's overgrown beak. When it came time to treat Bruta's bumble-foot, Corwyn taught me to hold her from behind—"mugging," he called it—and keep her still as he applied the salve. I felt the bird trembling in my arms, felt the quickened blood-beat in her breast. She tried to flap her wings, but I kept my arms clamped tightly about her and spoke to her in my mind. Gradually I felt her calm. When he had finished, Corwyn looked at me again in that measuring way of his but said nothing.

The sun had well risen when we had done, and still Corwyn had not made so much as a move toward the back mew. Now, I thought, we must surely begin work with the gyr. But there I mistook again. He motioned me to the workbench and set a piece of tanned goatskin before me. With a knife he scored the patterns for two jesses, with three slits in each one. "Cut these out," he said.

"But I thought," I said, "we were to work with the gyrfalcon today."

Corwyn, holding out the knife to me, looked mildly back, only hitching one dark eyebrow the tiniest bit. "All in good time," he said.

I swallowed my complaint, for I did not want to find myself back at tablet weaving again. I grasped the knife impatiently and tried to guide it along the scored lines, but this work was more irksome than it appeared. The knife slipped; it cut between the scores, and the jess was ruined.

I flung down the knife, crying, "I want to work with the gyr—not leather! You bade me come here early so we could work with her, and I have not so much as laid eyes on her. This leather work is more tedious than tablet weaving!"

Calmly, Corwyn bent to pick up the knife from the floor. "A falconer must learn to make his own equipage," he said levelly. "That is part of the art. Your bird will need jesses if you are to work with her." He held out the knife again.

I sighed and took back the knife, ashamed at my outburst. I concentrated hard on moving the blade along the scored lines and holding the leather so the knife wouldn't slip. Six jesses I ruined; after the fourth, Corwyn told me to remove my finger rings. I did so, and my circlet as well; Corwyn put them in a sack for safekeeping.

At last I had them, two thin leather jesses that met with Corwyn's approval. He showed me how to put them on a bird's leg, slipping one end of the jess through the middle slit and the other end through the slit on the first end, leaving the third slit free for attaching to a leash. I marveled how his huge hands could so easily do this fine work.

"I haven't jessed the gyr," he said, "because every time I come near she hurls herself against the walls. She's lunatic. The voyage was rough, and being pent up . . . some birds take it worse than others. But . . . do you think you can call her to fist as you did yesterday?"

"I think so."

"Then call, and if she comes, turn her away from me. I'll mug her from behind and you can jess her."

I hesitated. "Must we do it that way? She might . . . hold it against me."

"There *is* no other way with a wild bird, unless . . ." Corwyn considered. "Can you make her hold still while you jess her?"

"I can't make her," I said, "but perhaps she will be willing."

Corwyn appeared to weigh this in his mind. "Well, we will try your way," he said at last.

He handed me a glove; I put it on. As we approached the mew, he instructed me in a quiet voice: Know before you enter exactly where the bird is; keep your gloved hand before you and your eyes on the bird; shut the door behind you; if she should fly at you, protect your face with your glove.

I held my thoughts still as I opened the mew door. The gyr sidestepped along her perch, bobbing her head. I spoke to her softly as I shut the door behind me, then held out my gloved hand, my whole being concentrated upon her.

<Come.>

The mind-ripple again.

<Come.>

She looked straight at me, leaned forward, then she was sailing across the mew. I felt the weight of her as she alit, saw the life of her pulsing in her throat. I ached to ruffle her feathers but held back. She might consider that too familiar a gesture just yet. Her blue-black eyes gazed at me calmly; then abruptly she bent down and began cleaning her feet with her beak.

"So," Corwyn said softly.

I smiled, watching the gyr.

"I have spent days holding a wild bird with a piece of meat on my fist before the bird would trust me to look away from me and bend down to eat."

"I think . . . she can *feel* me," I said.

"So," Corwyn said again.

I reached for the jesses, tucked inside my sash. I pulled out the first one and tried with one hand to wrap it around her leg. My fingers felt clumsy, as if they were made of wood. The gyr cocked me a quizzical eye but did not otherwise protest. "I'm not very good at this," I said to her. "I'm not used to doing things with only one hand, and I'm clumsy at it." I didn't expect her to understand, exactly. I just felt like explaining it to her.

At last I managed to pull both ends through both slits. "This will be the last," I promised, taking out the second jess. The gyr stretched up and seemed to lean over to watch what I was doing but seemed not unduly concerned.

Around the leg, put the end through the slit . . . where was it, where was it? There. Now through the second slit, and cinch it in. There. Done.

I watched the gyr apprehensively, afraid she'd consider the jesses an affront.

She nibbled at them for a moment, more curious, it seemed, than vexed. She stretched up, looked at me. At last she made a sound deep in her throat—a sort of chuckling, a burbling sound. She fluffed out her feathers, then settled comfortably down upon my fist.

Chapter 9

By night the goddess Skava dons her cloak of
feathers and soars like a falcon through the sky.

—KRAGISH MYTH

A nd so I settled into the rhythm of the mews: Begin before
daylight, inspect and weigh the birds, put down fresh
sawdust, work with the gyr. Skava, I named her. At midday
Rath and Myrra always came from their lessons, bringing meat
and bread and cheese from the kitchenhouse. And afterward
we must go into the field and work the birds that had not been
taken up to hunt that day. Not Skava at first—she was not
yet ready.

We dared not dawdle over our meat for the days were
growing short. Darkness lingered well into the mornings and
crept back in before the evening meal. Soon snow lay thick
upon the land, pillowing in the needlecone trees, mounding
like bread loaves upon the steading roofs, making it impossible

to venture beyond courtyard and barnyard without shoebaskets or skis.

So we bolted the fare that Rath and Myrra brought, and tethered the birds to wicker cadging frames, and strapped on our shoebaskets. Then, with Corwyn carrying one frame and I the other, and Rath and Myrra lugging lures and gloves, we headed for the fields.

A few of the less reliable birds we flew with a creance—a long, thin line attached to the falconer's glove at one end and to the hawk's jesses at the other. This assured that the birds would not fly away. I would hold the hawk on my glove and then Corwyn would whistle, and the bird would fly from me to the meat on Corwyn's glove. Most of the time, that is. Sometimes a hawk flew off in another direction, or refused to fly at all. Yet on the return flight—from Corwyn to me—they nearly always came. At first, Corwyn insisted that I hold meat while calling them back, so as not to ruin their training. But after a time he laxed on this and let me summon them in my mind.

The better-trained birds we flew to the lure, a stuffed leather bag cut in the shape of a pigeon or duck. The lure was garnished with meat, attached to a long string, and swung in circles through the air. Someone—usually Rath or I—would release a bird at some distance; it would fly and attack the lure in midswing. Swinging the lure looked simple, but I found when I tried that there was a knack to it. And you had to do it one particular way for hawks and another way altogether for falcons.

At day's end we four would sit round the fire in the mews, sipping a warm, sweet brew of milk and spices. Corwyn, Rath, and I repaired leashes and hoods and other leather gear.

Sometimes I practiced the falconer's knot that Corwyn had taught me to tie with one hand only. Myrra would settle down on the rushes, lean back against Corwyn's legs, and make birds and animals out of clay. Before long, Skava had become so easy with me that she perched upon my shoulder—sometimes napping, sometimes nibbling at my hair, sometimes chiming into the conversation with a companionable burble. I sat in the flickering light, those evenings, breathing in the smoky, leather-and-sawdust-scented air, letting the sensations wash over me: tiredness, warmth, and an odd, unaccustomed feeling of content.

From time to time Kazan would come and sit with us. Mostly he talked with Corwyn—about ships, about their home countries, about capturing and trading hawks. The king, it seemed, pressed Kazan to stay on and be his shipbuilder, but Kazan kept saying no. "This cold," he said. "What fool would *choose* to live in this cold?" Corwyn shrugged and smiled ruefully, for he was compelled to stay here, as was I. Still, Corwyn seemed to like Kazan and heartily welcomed him when he came.

Kazan never spoke to me again about calling down birds, although I was prepared in case he did. I had practiced in my mind the cold stare that I would give him and was almost disappointed that I didn't have to use it. Indeed, Kazan hardly spoke to me. Nor did I enter into the talk when he came, but found myself drawn against my will by his stories of faraway places and adventures at sea. My glance strayed, those winter evenings, across his saffron-colored boots, to the charms on his sash, to the triangle of light above his high, flat cheekbones.

But just before he left, Kazan always asked me about Skava. He could *see* her well enough upon my shoulder, yet always he asked how her training went and if she were content.

72

And always I felt the heat of his gaze upon me. The words, when I answered him, oft went awry in my mouth. And I was glad that the hearth companions were not there to see this, for they would have misconstrued, and taken up their irksome hooting.

My work with Skava went slowly at first. Not because of her—because of Corwyn. Before he would allow me to fly her, he insisted I spend time simply carrying her about the steading on my fist. I was to keep her with me nearly all the time, going to meals with her, and even tethering her to my bedpost at night. Manning the bird, he called it. I did as he wished, except that I would not force her to wear a hood. She tolerated the jesses—even the brass bells I tethered to her legs—but she bit and struck with her feet at the hood as if she considered it an affront.

During the first few days she would often fly off my wrist in alarm at the sight of a man or a dog or a horse. Bating, Corwyn called it. She could not fly in this wise more than a fingerlength, for I held onto her jesses, but she beat furiously at the air with her wings, and I could feel the cold trickle of her rage at me for holding her. I stopped and spoke to her softly when she did this, waiting for her to subside. At last she would stop flapping her wings and let herself fall and hang upside down by her jesses. Then I cradled her breast gently in my right hand and helped her back onto my left wrist.

My left arm perpetually ached.

Walking through the steading with Skava, I marked a change in the way folk regarded me. Ever since the dove-calling the common folk had treated me with deference. "Lady Kara," they would say, and yield to me as I passed. But now they looked curiously at Skava and nodded and smiled at me. Young children trooped about me, gaping up at Skava and asking me all about her. She enthralled them, much more so than the many other trained falcons on the steading. Perhaps it was her whiteness—which was indeed rare—or perhaps her fame, since the king had given her to me. Or perhaps, I thought darkly, it was that they expected her to help me call down dragons. Even the hearth companions came to look at Skava, although they remained aloof to me. "Everybody loves you," I said to Skava, scratching her head and throat. She ruffled her feathers complacently, accepting my praise as her due.

The dragon hunt! If only it weren't for that! For I was happy here—happier than ever I had been at home. My mother and my father loved me—that I knew—and my brothers also. But as for the others . . .

Here, among folk who held me in esteem, I realized for the first time what a burden it had been to live despised by some and feared by most of the rest.

Still, the prospect of this dragon hunt shadowed me everywhere and dimmed my new content. Orrik had put out a call for warriors, and now they began to arrive. Only a trickle at first: groups of three or four men. But the trickle swelled to a flood, and soon every spare span of storehouse filled up with warriors and their gear. Warriors crowded the bench-space in the hall and, as the days grew cold and dark, spilled over into a village of tents in the courtyard. By day the sky was streaked by the smokes of their fires; by night their lanterns lumined eddies of skurreling snow. The air echoed with the shouts of many men, the clopping of many horses, and the shrill, ringing clangor that sounded all day from the forge.

You will call down dragons for the king.

Dragons . . .

Many strong men had been killed by dragons. Their

breathfire, I had heard, was hotter than the hottest forge; they were seven times taller than the tallest horse; their teeth and claws made a wolf pack seem benign. The very thought of calling dragons brought a sickening flood of fear up through my lungs to my throat.

And yet . . . it was nearly as bad, when I thought of this dragon hunt, to imagine them *not* coming to my call. It would be a . . . disgrace. Folk would glare at me and whisper behind my back as they did in my home steading. The king might send me home in shame.

It *was* pleasing, being well thought of. And how much more pleasing if I should prove myself a heroine. Often and often my thoughts strayed into daytime dreams of calling down dragons and purging the land of them, of winning the king's gratitude and the adulation of the folk. Sometimes, in my imaginings, I returned to my father's steading in a triumphal procession, and even my aunt knelt before me.

At last the day came when Corwyn said that Skava was ready to be flown free. We had begun inside the mews, flying her from me to Corwyn, then back again when I called <Come.> Then we worked her outdoors in the afternoons with a creance line, first flying her fist to fist and then short distances to the lure. She learned quickly.

And so this day I took up Skava from the cadge and walked alone with her to the top of a snowy knoll. We ventured farther afield these days—up into the fells to the north—to avoid the commotion at the steading. Corwyn stood at some distance with the lure; our plan was to have Skava fly once to the lure and reward her and then go home.

But Skava had other ideas.

"You *wouldn't* fly away, would you?" I asked her as I loosed her jesses from my glove. She looked at me with a direct, impenetrable gaze, then turned and seemed to devour the landscape with her blue-black eyes. My heart was pounding; I was terrified. But Corwyn said it was always thus the first time a hawk flew free.

Skava roused, muted, cast off. She flew directly toward the lure, and I breathed a sigh of relief. But too soon. At the last instant she veered away from Corwyn, came circling around, and made a low pass farther away, just above Rath and Myrra.

I lost sight of her for a moment as she circled again. Then the jingling of bells caught my ear; I looked around to see her flying straight at me, her eyes intent upon my face. I froze; she passed me so nearly by that I swear I felt a feather brush my cheek.

"What are you *doing?*" I muttered.

And then she began to climb.

She arced out and up, to come overhead, then began ringing up and up into the darkening winter sky. The sound of her bells broke the silence and then gradually faded as she ringed higher and still higher, until I could see no more of her than a tiny white flickering of wings.

I felt a fluttering of fear in my breast. She was free now; she could leave if she chose. "Shall I call her?" I shouted to Corwyn.

"Not yet," he said. "I'll swing the lure."

But at that moment a snow grouse thundered up out of the underbrush near Rath.

"Ho!" Corwyn shouted. "Ho!"

There was a faint sizzling noise in the air high above me.

76

I looked up to see Skava stooping to the earth: an arrow point, a teardrop shape, a bird with folded wings. The sizzling built to a whooshing roar, and then . . . *thud*! An explosion of feathers as she hit her quarry. Skava pitched up sharply, looking back over her shoulder at the dropping snow grouse, then swung around and settled down upon her prey.

I stood dazed for a moment. Then I roused myself and sprinted—clumsy, in my shoebaskets—down the knoll toward Skava. I found her neatly plucking out the snow grouse's thigh feathers. She raised her head and silently hissed at my approach. Corwyn, Rath, and Myrra soon joined me; no one spoke.

I let Skawa fill her crop, then held out my arm. She jumped to my wrist without complaint. Long purplish shadows stretched across the snowy hills; a solitary star hung low in the sky. And I was flooded with awe: awe at the flight, awe at the death, awe that this splendid creature would consent to share it with me.

Nothing could surpass that flight, I thought. But that very evening, something nearly did. The four of us were sitting in the mews—Corwyn, Rath, Myrra, and I. Skava perched upon a wooden barrel while I repaired a swivel for her leash. My fingers slipped, and one of the metal rings went flying. I could see it glinting in the stray lamplight, just beyond my reach. My muscles were sore from a hard day's working, and I felt too tired even to get up off my bench. "If only you would go fetch me that ring, you lazy bird," I said to Skava in jest. She pushed off the barrel, sailed low across the room, and alit upon the ring.

I stared.

It is true that I spoke often to Skava, but it was as with any animal: more for the tone of it than for the meaning of the words. The only word she understood, I thought, was the <come> when I summoned, spoken inside me in a concentrating way, with a certain force of will. But now . . . Could she have understood me?

I slipped on a gauntlet and summoned, <Come!> Skava flew back across the mews and landed on my wrist. She did not have the ring; it still glimmered in the sawdust on the floor.

"She didn't fetch it."

Myrra had stopped working with her clay and was gazing up at me. "She flew to the ring but didn't fetch it," she said.

I nodded. Now Corwyn and Rath looked questioningly at us.

"I—I am going to try something," I said.

I concentrated hard on the ring and said, <Go,> in my mind. I tried to *feel* that "go," to summon all my will and channel it in the direction of the ring.

Skava pushed off my wrist, glided down, and landed again on the ring.

Excitement pounded in my veins.

"What happened, then?" Corwyn asked.

"I think I am . . . directing her," I said. I summoned Skava back, then scanned the room, looking for another place she might fly to. The door to her mew was ajar, barely visible in the gloom. "I'll try sending her to her mew," I said.

<Your mew,> I thought. <Go.>

Skava ducked her head between her legs and peered up at me.

<Go,> I repeated.

She scratched her chin indifferently with the sharp talon of one toe.

Disappointment flooded me. "I guess it was a fluke," I said.

"Try another place," Corwyn suggested. "Something shiny like the ring. That bell on the workbench, perhaps?"

A small brass bell, the kind we tied on falcons' legs, twinkled on the workbench in the light of the lamp. I looked at it, concentrating hard, and said, <Go,> in the willful way.

Skava pushed off my wrist and alit upon the bell.

"So," Corwyn said, arching his brows. He glanced at me again in that way of his, part appraising, part marveling. "This is . . . interesting."

I tried directing Skava to other places as well. She wouldn't fly to the ones I could not see well. And she never did fetch. But she flew to a brass scale and to a silver coin and to a falconer's glove. The glove interested Corwyn, for all the other things she had flown to were shiny. "This . . . directing you do," he said, "is unlike anything I have ever seen or heard of. It is . . . a wonder. I would like to know," he said thoughtfully, "how far you can direct her, and to what sorts of things she will fly. What say we take her out into the field early, without the other birds, and try this? I am eager to learn what she will do."

"And I also."

"And I," Rath said. "I want to see, too!"

"Me, too! Me, too!" Myrra echoed.

"Very well," Corwyn said. "On the morrow, we will take our suppers to the northern fells."

"I can fetch trinkets for her to fly to," Rath said.

"I can fetch berry cakes," Myrra put in.

"I think I can get Gudjen to lend us hides to sit on," I said.

"You fetch Skava," Corwyn said. "I'll mind the hides."

Such were the plans we made—but a summons from the king put an end to them all.

Chapter 10

And you shall have diversities of gifts,
some with strings tied to them, some without.

—THE GODDESS SKAVA TO FIRST WOMAN,
KRAGISH MYTH

I t came in the early dark of the next morning. I awoke to
someone shaking me and the light of an oil lamp slickering
across my bedcurtains. Gudjen was saying my name.

"Kara, wake up," she said. "The king would see you
now."

"The king?" I asked, stupid with sleep.

"He would have words with you—now, before the household wakes. Dress yourself. I will come when you have done
and lead you to him."

Dread lay heavy in my chest. *The dragon hunt.* Reluctantly, I pushed back the quilts and let the chill air wash over
me. I drew on my shift, my best gown, my red cape, then
bent to pull on my boots.

Skava was still sleeping, one foot tucked up beneath her and the other clutching my bedpost. Most days she woke me with her noisy rousing and stretching; it must truly be early now. "Wake up," I said, drawing on my gauntlet. I unleashed her from my bedpost, ruffling her breast feathers as I took her up. She looked about sleepily. "The king wants to see us," I told her. "Look alert."

Gudjen led us past the row of curtained beds, past the sleeping bondmaids on their pallets, and out into the courtyard.

Cold engulfed us in a wave. The sky was softly dark and freckled with stars. Yet the pale, watery light of the moon infused the air, illuminating my puffs of breath and the snow-thatched buildings beyond. We followed Gudjen—one never walked *with* Gudjen, but always followed—over the hard-packed snow in the courtyard toward the high hall. To my surprise we continued past it and turned onto a narrow, trampled track that led through the snow to a stand of birches.

The king was there, waiting. He wore no crown, yet still looked kingly in his fur-lined cloak, with gold glinting at his fingers. His wolfhound rose at our approach, ears pricked.

"Thank you, my sister," the king said to Gudjen; then, to me, "Kara."

I executed a one-handed curtsey, for Skava was perched on my left wrist.

"How goes it with—what have you named the bird?" he asked.

I had told him twice before: once, at evening meat, when I had thanked him for her, and another time when he had spoken to me in the courtyard. But the king no doubt had too much on his mind to recall such trifling matters.

"Skava," I said and added, "It goes . . . well," not quite

understanding what he wished to know. "And I thank you again for her; she is—"

He waved my thanks aside. "Do not thank me. She is what they call a king's gift, a gift with obligations tied to it. As you have no doubt surmised." He smiled—a tired smile, I thought. He held out his hand for me to precede him along the track.

"Come back to me when you have done," Gudjen called.

The track, I saw, curved down beyond the birches and then up again into the grazing land above the steading until it lost itself in shadow. Orrik ceded the trodden part to me and broke his own way in the crusted snow beside, while his hound ranged along before us. The king asked if my sleeping quarters suited me and if I liked my work in the mews and if the company of Corwyn pleased me. I answered briefly, for I knew that this was courtesy only and that his real purpose in calling me lay elsewhere.

After a while his questions dwindled. He stopped at a rocky outcrop and stood for a time looking north to where mountains shouldered into fields of pale stars. Below us lay the valley, lumined in moonlight, smoothed by snow into gentle mounds and hollows.

The air was sharp and chill. Skava stirred upon my wrist.

"On the morrow we leave to hunt dragons," Orrik said. "I and my warriors . . . and you."

There was a stillness in me. I had known this, after all.

The king turned to me. "I tell you truly, Kara, I do not know how to find them. How shall we go about it?"

I stared at him, too startled, for a moment, to speak. At last I said, "But I thought that they were there." I pointed to the distant mountains. "I thought those were the dragonlands."

"We know the dragons are thereabouts. Or were, in any case. For that is where Signy's brother met his death. Yet those mountains encompass a vast territory.

"My advisers—" The king sighed. "My . . . *brother* advises me that now is the best time for a dragon hunt. The dragons, bedrowsed in their winter lairs, Rog claims, can be jolted out of sleep by the clash of swords on shields. They fly"—here the king moved his hand up in the air in imitation of a flying dragon—"fly before they come fully awake, and thus are easily slain.

"Yet before you came, when we traveled to the dragonlands, we roused no dragons. We *saw* no dragons. Rog says we had not men enough; it was not yet winter; the dragons were still awake and could not be startled. But I do not know. Dragons are wily creatures, and it may be that this way is of no use." The king, intent now, leaned toward me. His eyes, though feathered with creases, were clear blue and penetrating. "And so, Kara," he said, "I ask again. How shall we go about it?"

It was frightening to have him speak to me in this wise. It was most unkinglike. I had preferred to think he knew what he was about, even when it meant I had to do something I did not wish to. Even though I was afraid.

If the king had no better plan than this, and all of it rested upon me . . . I felt my foolish dreams of glory shrink and fade.

"My king," I said, "I do not know! I know nothing of dragons. I have never *seen* a dragon. I know there is a story they tell of me and a dragon and her cave, but I remember none of it."

He rubbed his beard thoughtfully. I could not tell

whether he were angry or no. "And yet," he said, "you call down winged things from the sky."

"Birds," I said. "Never dragons."

"Some say that birds and dragons are akin. They say that if you can call one, you can also call the other. And then there is . . . Skava, you have named her?"

I nodded. Skava roused on my wrist and looked at me as if she knew we spoke of her. Absently, I scratched her feet.

"Perhaps," Orrik said, "she can sense them. Falcons do, they say. Perhaps she can—in the way she has of communing with you—tell you where they are." He paused. "You do commune with each other, do you not? When you call her, she comes?"

"Yes, but—"

Orrik interrupted impatiently. "Gudjen has seen it in the steam that you will summon dragons for me—and the steam does not lie." He seemed displeased with me. His hound, pacing restlessly beside him, rumbled in its throat.

"I saw what Gudjen worked in the steam," I said carefully, "and I know she believes I can call dragons. But, your grace, I cannot even call an eagle and make it come!"

"You *will* make them come," Orrik said. "How, I do not know, and perhaps you do not either, but you will! It's in the steam!" He began to pace, then stopped abruptly. "Are you afraid? Is that it?"

"Well, yes, but—"

"I will ring you round with archers. You won't be in the fray." He went on pacing, mapping out plans to keep me safe. He would post twenty archers to every dragon; they would form an impenetrable wall; if any dragon came near me, he would shield me from it with his own body. He said something about fishnets and a trap.

"But—" I hesitated. "But what if I can't find them? What if I call and they don't come? And all the warriors will be there waiting, and everything riding on it . . ."

I had hoped he would reassure me, tell me I could only try. Instead, he looked out toward the mountains again. When he turned to me, his face was grave.

"Kara," he said, "you *will* do this. I *need* you. If I march my warriors through the snow, foeless, they will lose heart and mutter against me. If I fail to carry out Signy's blood feud, I will have forsworn myself; I will lose her hand, and her father may well declare war. If I fail to stem the dragon raids, the folk will turn against me. And Rog . . . well, I fear what he will do. This is a test of my power—a test of *me*. If I fail in this, my kingdom will come unraveled, and all that I have worked for will crumble away."

I felt the weight of it upon my shoulders—the weight of two kingdoms. I groped about in my mind for another way, a way out. It seemed unwise—*unfair*—to lay the whole of the burden on me, with such thin signs that I could help. "Maybe the—the shields," I stammered, "the beaten shields . . ."

Orrik said nothing. His eyes did not leave my face. I wanted nothing more than to break away and run—run across the fells and away. But there was no hiding from this.

"I will . . . try," I whispered at last.

I was not allowed to go to the mews that day. I tethered Skava to my bedpost while Gudjen bustled me about the steading, making preparations for my journey. I followed her from storehouse to storehouse, accumulating provisions: two down coverlets, a bearskin, three fur-lined cloaks, two spare pairs of boots, skins for a tented booth.

I fretted so to be allowed to talk to Corwyn about Skava that Gudjen sent a messenger to him. Later that day, as I watched the sled being loaded in the courtyard—housecarls and bondmaids bustling about surrounded by a horde of children and dogs, with Gudjen presiding all over—I felt a tugging at my sleeve. I turned around to see Rath grinning at me, Corwyn and Myrra beside him.

"You need not worry overmuch about Skava," Corwyn said, "for she is born to the cold. If it storms, stow her inside your cloak, but other times she will be well. I brought you mice to feed her"—he handed me a large packet—"but if these are not enough, I'll wager she can hunt for herself."

Then Rath said, "Hold out your hands, Kara, and close your eyes."

"Not more dead mice, I hope."

"Discover for yourself," he said. "Hold out your hands."

Smiling, I did as he bade me. There was a jingle, and two round things dropped into my hands. I opened my eyes and beheld two silver bells—attached to thin leather bewits.

"These are beautiful!" I said. "Much more beautiful than the brass ones Skava has now."

"I made the bewits myself," Rath said, drawing himself up proudly. "And . . . someone gave me the bells, for Skava."

"Kazan did!" Myrra said.

"Shush! You weren't supposed to tell!" Rath admonished Myrra. "You promised."

Myrra stuck out her lower lip, abashed. "I forgot," she said.

"You did not—you just *wanted* to tell."

"Did so! I did so forget!"

Rath sighed, exasperated. "Kara, please don't tell Kazan you know. I promised I would keep it a secret, but *some folk* can't seem to do so."

"I *forgot*," Myrra said, lower lip trembling.

Rath sighed again.

Corwyn smiled, laid a hand on Myrra's shoulder. "Give Kara what you worked for her," he said.

Myrra perked up. "Hold out your hand and close your eyes!" she said. "Maybe it's a dead mouse!"

I held out my hands and felt something rounded and solid drop into them.

When I opened my eyes I saw that it was one of her clay makings, sculpted in the shape of a small bird. I knew it was a kestrel, but was not sure exactly how I knew. It was crudely formed and rough-edged and lopsided and glazed a strange purplish green, but there was something of *kestrelness* about it.

"This is beautiful," I said to Myrra.

All at once she was hugging me, burying her head in my skirts, and a lump was rising in my throat.

Corwyn leaned over Myrra to clap me roughly on the shoulders. "Until we meet," he said. "I will not say farewell." He pried Myrra away and, hoisting her up, lumbered off toward the mews.

Rath stood awkwardly, looking as if he did not know whether to hug me or clap my shoulders or shake my hand. "Those dragons better watch out because you're going to . . . well, you and Skava, you'll . . ." Whatever he was about to say fizzled in his mouth; he turned on his heel and fled.

I stood watching as they left, with the chaos of preparations going on all around me and a chaos of feeling inside.

These are my friends, I thought. There was an aching in my chest—an odd aching—which felt bad and good at once.

Later that day, long after the sun had traced its shallow arc above the horizon, Gudjen led me to the steamhouse. It was dark, save for a fire in the hearthpit, which she had started earlier. I tethered Skava to a perch near the door. Gudjen took a torch from a cresset in the wall, lighted it in the fire, then went round the room lighting all the torches, until shadow upon shadow leapt upon the walls. She shut the smokehole, blotting out the square of stars. Then she went about as she had done the day I came, pouring water onto the hot, smooth stones.

This time it happened almost at once.

There was a hissing explosion of steam, and another and another, all massed together to form a billowing cloud. The cloud spread out, thinned, shredded into coiling ribbons that unraveled in the flickering torchlight, then seemed to gather into sinuous strands of tail and wing and claw. And a circle of steamy dragons glared down at me, transparent to the torches, pulsing their wings, rippling as if stirred by an unseen breeze.

Sweat trickled down my face; my robe clung wet to my body. The air was hot and heavy and hard to breathe.

All at once, Skava cried and bated off her perch—no, not bated—she was loose—she was flying. The steam-dragons stretched out, then one by one peeled away from the walls to trail behind Skava as she flew. They blurred around the edges and then slowly broke up, like curdling milk.

Where was Skava? I strained to pick out her solid form among the steam-shapes but could not.

And now the steam seemed to be gathering itself into a

new shape—a squat, blocky mountain peak from which issued a cloudy plume. I minded me at once of the land of many smokes that Kazan had told me of. Skava's land.

And still I could not see her!

<Skava! Come!>

She flew right *through* the mountain—punched a ragged hole in it—and landed on my bare fist.

Her talons pricked my flesh but did not dig in. I stroked her breast and spoke to her softly. Skava burbled in her throat, gently nibbling my fingers. I heard Gudjen opening the door and smokehole, felt the air grow cool and thin, but did not look up.

"I thought I lost you!" I said. It was foolish, I knew—for where could she have gone?

And yet my heart still beat wildly in my throat. If ever she were lost . . .

But I would not think of that now.

Chapter 11

For fending off the bite of frost:
a thick fur,
a bright fire,
a fast friend.

—KRAGISH PROVERB

There was revelry in the high hall that night. Orrik took me up beside him on the dais and spoke in ringing tones to the warriors gathered below. Torchlight blazed in my eyes so that I could not well behold the men who, reeking of brew, cheered and clashed sword against shield at Orrik's every pause for breath.

And early the next morning we gathered in the courtyard to depart.

A hubbub of children and dogs, of bondmaids and craftsmen and noblewomen, flocked round the troop of warriors. Although the sun would not rise for a long while yet, the courtyard was stippled with light: the flares from many torches, the moonlit fogs of many breaths. Sweethearts draped warstrips, red ribbons cut from wadmal cloth, about the shoulders of their men, for luck. All of the warriors—including me, including even the king—wore packs bulging with provisions. The men bristled with bows and quivers, with swords and shields and war axes that thumped and clanked as they made their way on ski through the courtyard.

The largest dogs on the steading had been commandeered as pack animals; they milled about like strange, humped beasts. There was but a single dogsled, for equipage only: the king's tent and the cook's provisions and what seemed a landkir of fishnetting. Yet Gudjen had managed to get my tent and some extra furs and boots stowed away on it as well.

I stood somewhat apart, with Skava on my wrist. The cold air burned my face. This festive mood washed over me, leaving me untouched, like rain on sealskin. I looked about for Corwyn and Rath and Myrra but could not find them. Kazan I saw talking to a hearth companion; he turned as I watched, hesitated, then seemed to move toward me. But at that moment the king emerged from a group of well-wishers and motioned me to come.

"Here we go," I said under my breath to Skava as we hastened toward the king. He stepped up onto the loaded sled and pulled me up beside him. Skava let out a little squawk in protest, then subsided and looked curiously about.

Orrik began to speak to the gathered folk. His words told of blood feuds, vengeance, a stirring venture, and cleaning out the nest of vipers. He spoke of his impending marriage and the future line of Kragland. No word did he utter of his doubts. And I felt strangely alone, as if everyone about me listened to a stirring harpsong, but only I could hear the ominous counterpoint of thunder rolling in the mountains.

Then the king clasped me on the shoulders and leaned in close. "May fortune attend us—both of us!" he said in a low, intent voice, and I knew he heard the thunder, too. Then he jumped off the sled and helped me down. At once Skava and I were besieged by a troop of children; they draped me with red war-strips until I could not move without shedding. Here was something of the glory I had craved: the war-strips, the adulation. And yet it only increased my unease, for I had not earned it. Perhaps *could* not earn it. I spoke quietly to Skava, afraid that she would bate. She flapped her wings and gave a short, protesting squawk, but otherwise seemed calm enough, even when one child draped a war-strip about her neck. She tolerated this for a moment, then impatiently tossed it off.

Before long the crowd in the courtyard began to shift in a purposeful way; the warriors were assembling themselves into a column, with the king and his hearth companions at the head and other soldiers after. I stood aside, uncertain, not knowing where my place should be, until Gudjen gripped me by the elbow and propelled me to the head of the column. "You belong *here,*" she said. "By the king."

Orrik gave a great shout, which was echoed by his hearth companions; we set off through the courtyard. Weapons jinked and clanked; folk waved and shouted farewells. I schussed with the king through the courtyard, around the side of the high hall, up the path. When we reached the rocky outcrop, I turned and looked back. The long line of warriors, pricked by torchlight, runneled out from the lighted courtyard and wound over the hills like a stream from a calm summer lake.

We were three days on ski to the mountains. At first there was a gay mood to our party. The warriors sang bawdy songs and laughed uproariously, shedding war-strips as they walked, like a flock of duck in molt. Although the hearth

93

companions tolerated my presence, none spoke to me directly. I sensed that many thought I did not belong on this hunt—much less in the vanguard with them. They tolerated me because of the king. "I'm an interloper in their exalted ranks," I murmured to Skava.

Some of the men seemed to go out of their way to devise ribald lyrics to discomfit me. Rog especially encouraged them—but kept a safe distance from Skava.

Kazan, I saw, did not join in the singing; but neither did he approach me. The king had left my side to discuss urgent matters with his advisers and so paid no heed to me either.

"He's not my nursemaid," I told Skava. "Why should he protect me from his own hearth companions?"

Gudjen had bade me stay close to Orrik—this, not for my safety, but to preserve my status. Yet I found I did not want to hang about him like a lovesick puppy; nor did I wish to encourage those uncouth ballad singers by blushing at their songs.

"I can't bear much more of this, Skava, can you?" I said. Skava burbled to me and gently nibbled at my fingers. I let the vanguard pass me by and settled at last into walking near the rear of the column, by the dogsled. Gudjen would have had fits had she known.

Before long my left arm grew tired and cramped from holding Skava; I tied her jesses to the sledge. She rode along cheerfully, her wings fully extended as she breasted the breeze.

The first day we walked through farmland—rolling hills dotted by freeborn steaders' houses and byres. That night we stayed at a farmstead.

The next day the steadings grew more sparse; that night

we camped sheltered by a stand of birch trees. By the third day all joviality had trailed off as we settled into the grueling, hard drudgery of snow travel. Although walking had warmed my blood before, now cold crept into my toes and feet and would not leave. From time to time I heard laughter or a burst of song from the hearth companions up ahead, but mostly they had fallen silent. The sled runners scraped as they bit through the hard snow crust. The dogs panted, their muzzles rimy white, their harness bells jangling. Yet these sounds had a surface quality to them, amid a deepening silence.

Now we walked through a hushed world that admitted no sign of human occupation other than ourselves: a world of needlecone forests and rocky scaurs, of snow-drifted meadows and lonely alpine lakes. Sometimes we saw ravens or redpoll, rabbit tracks or wolf sign; once I even saw a gray gyr. But never any humans. None but us.

The sun tipped above the horizon for only a short time each day, and yet its light lingered long hours in the southern sky: streaks of violet and cobalt and purple, all above a gleaming rim of gold. Stars clustered thickly above us. The waxing moon rose early and set late, bathing the snowy landscape in milky blue light, so that we could see for many landkir without torches.

Yet the mountains to which we trekked were dark. They had grown until they blocked out the sky ahead of us, until we trod upon their roots. And I could not see the tops of them; they were shrouded in billowing clouds. It seemed we traveled away from the territories of light into a dark country, far from the shining fjords and the comfortable steading houses. There was an ominous feel to this place, as if it were inhabited by the ancient gods, the gods before our gods.

Late in the day I began to tire. I had tired before, but the tiredness of one day seemed to add itself to the tiredness of the others, and this time I felt that I could not go on much longer. My legs hurt; my breath came ragged and fast. Snow was falling now, pelting my face. My feet felt frigid, but I could no longer feel my toes; they clumped along inside my boots like chunks of wood.

I looked ahead at the mountains no more, but, head down, saw only my breath-mist and the whirling snow before me. The dogsled—with Skava on it—and most of the men had passed me by. On the other days I had caught up to them when they stopped to clear the dogs' feet of ice, but now I lagged too far behind. I trudged along in the hindmost fringe of stragglers, trying to quell my unreasonable stirrings of resentment against Orrik for not coming to see to my welfare, or at least sending someone else. *You think the king has nothing more to do than to nursemaid you?* But then I heard a voice beside me—"Kara?"—and I looked up, startled.

It was Kazan.

"Are you—" he began, and then was silent for a moment. "Can I carry something for you?" he asked at last.

The tears took me by surprise. I felt them welling up, stinging behind my nose and eyes, and I bit my lip hard to keep them back.

I shook my head, not looking at him.

I waited for him to leave, yet the schuss of his skis continued; I could see them moving in the snow beside mine.

"You don't like me," he said at last.

Jolted, I looked up at him, then away. I shrugged.

"You think," Kazan said, "that I would use you to entrap birds so that I might enrich myself."

This time I looked at him longer. "Wouldn't you?" I asked.

Kazan appeared to consider. "If you would *like* to do so, I would be pleased."

I hastened forward, away from him.

"*But,*" Kazan said, catching up to me, "if you would not—I would not ask it."

I said nothing, but only thrust one ski after the other through the snow.

"You don't believe me," Kazan said.

"Why should I?"

Again Kazan appeared to consider. "Because it's true," he said. He opened his coat and began fumbling for something in his sash. "Now I would like to give you a gift with no obligations tied to it," he said. At once I recalled the bells— the silver falcon bells he had given for Skava—and I was a little ashamed of my rudeness.

"No," I said, and added, "thank you."

But Kazan was already holding out something in his hand. It was, I saw, a dried yellow fruit, of the sort I had tried once at home. My foolish mouth began to water.

"I like to give these to you northerners," Kazan said. "I like to see your faces when you eat something with *flavor* to it."

"Our food has flavor enough," I said. "I tried one of these fruits another time, and it was . . . too sweet."

"Too *sweet?* You northerners know nothing of sweet. Your cursed cold *scares* the sweetness out of everything."

"Maybe you are so sated with cloying sweets that you have no palate for other flavors."

This time it was Kazan who shrugged. "If you don't want it, I will go." He kept his gloved hand out, offering the fruit.

I hesitated. The fruit looked soft and moist and succulent. Again I thought of the bells, which he had not wanted me to know he gave. I reached for the fruit. "You can stay," I said, as if it did not matter one way or the other.

The fruit suffused my mouth with a delicious sweetness. I allowed myself to smile.

Chapter 12

*And if your bird grows rapt upon your fist
and neither rouses nor eats nor flies—
beware, for there be dragons about.*

—THE FALCONER'S ART

That night we made camp in a canyon. It was a dark, forbidding place with high, sloping walls threaded through at the bottom by a river locked in ice. No longer could we see the mountains before us; we were among them.

The dragonlands, I thought, watching Skava. She sat tense upon my fist, as if listening. To what? Could it be dragons?

We had entered the canyon late in the day, gliding along the snow-shrouded river. The king and hearth companions seemed to know this place, for I heard someone call, "See there! Ahead!" and all stopped and looked up through the falling snow to the canyon wall, where a ledge of rock overhung a recessed groove.

Although it was not a difficult climb on foot, the dogs

couldn't pull the sled up the slope. We had unloaded it, taken off our skis, and packed in food and provisions. Kazan's companions had whistled and hooted as he helped me haul my blankets and sleeping robes. He made a rude gesture in their direction, then grinned and shrugged at me.

It was a shallow cave, this place where we camped—only as deep as two men laid head to foot—yet it was so long that all of our number could comfortably fit. I tethered Skava to a tree root that clutched at the overhanging ledge just above the place where I would sleep. She paid me no mind but continued staring up the canyon, listening. I wished I knew what she heard. I wished I knew how to find the dragons through her, as the king seemed to expect me to do.

I sat around one of the campfires with Kazan and some younger hearth companions whom he had befriended. We talked quietly in the dark, supping on cold dried fish and bread.

Fear had come to stand like a shadow beside me. Though I talked and ate and even laughed at times, it ever lurked around the corners of my eyes.

Orrik moved among the clusters of men, pausing to say a word of encouragement here or answer a query there. When he came to our fire, he stopped and sat by me. He told us of the plan, which had been rumored about camp: I would stand on the frozen river and call the dragons, using Skava however I might. They would fly down into the canyon; the walls would funnel them to the fore of the archers, who would shoot them down from beneath the ledge.

"The canyon will act as a chute, their death trap," Orrik said. He turned to me. "There were but five of them that Signy's father saw, and we have a hundred archers. Twenty archers to each dragon! And you will stand downriver from us, so the dragons will be dead before ever they come near you."

"But the fishnets?" I asked. "How will you use them?"

"We have no need of them in this place, Kara." Then, sensing my uncertainty, he went on, "Never fear. I would not put you in the way of danger for a hundred kingdoms." He clasped my shoulder and looked into my eyes, yet a mutinous thought whispered in my mind: He *was* endangering me, and protesting that he was not did not change it.

B reakfast was more cold dried fish and another hunk of frozen bread. I ate quickly, trying to numb my fear and simply *act*. It was too late to go back. What would come, would come.

While I was feeding Skava, Orrik approached. He waited until I finished, then wrapped me about with the skin of a great white bear and led me to a place beneath the ledge where his hearth companions were gathered.

"She goes now," he told them. "Take your places."

I breathed in deep and would have started down the slope were it not that a firm hand on my arm detained me. I turned around and found myself looking straight into Kazan's eyes. Dark eyes: grave, intent. He pressed a cluster of the yellow dried fruits into my hand. I nodded, stuffed the fruits into my sash, then turned to go.

It was only when I was partway down the slope that I realized that no one had hooted.

All our bootprints and skiprints and dogprints and stumbleprints had vanished beneath the powdery tarp left by last night's snowfall. Fear lurked at the corners of my eyes again, but I warded it off by trying to guess where, beneath the snow, the footholds were. The moon laid long black shadows across the slope. Many times I nearly fell, and once I did slip and came down hard on my side. Skava flapped her wings to stay upright and favored me with an irritated squawk.

"I'd like to see *you* walk down this slope," I told her, but she paid me no mind—only resumed her rapt watchfulness.

I trudged slowly out onto the river, listening for the squeak of cracking ice, feeling for a shifting underfoot. It was foolish, I knew; the ice had been strong enough yesterday to hold an army. Yet attending to the ice kept the darker fear at bay.

Downriver, the king had said.

I walked until I was below the downriver tip of the ledge.

"Well, Skava," I said, "here we go."

I stood facing upriver and called, <Come,> as if I were summoning a bird. It was silent, eerily silent, standing there in that canyon where nothing moved, where even the water was locked in ice. Deep in the shadows beneath the ledge I could make out the tiny forms of men. The sloping rock walls framed a dark strip of sky, where cloudy patches cobbled over the glimmering stars.

<Come,> I called. <Come.>

In the distance I heard the cry of a bird, then another and another. Now I saw them coming down the canyon—two ravens, a redpoll, a wind gull—and a terrible thought seized me. What if all the birds from miles around came while I was calling dragons? I would make a laughable spectacle, dragged down by the weight of a hundred birds!

Yet these birds did not approach too near but circled lazily overhead.

I had expected Skava to become excited at the sight of the other birds—perhaps to bate off my fist. But she hardly deigned to glance at them. She stood still and intent, staring up the canyon.

<Come,> I called.

No dragons. All was silent, save for the calls of the circling birds.

I took in a deep breath, torn between relief and disappointment.

Perhaps I was going about this wrongly. Perhaps I should make it clear that this call was to *dragons* and not birds. <Come, dragons!> I called.

Nothing.

<Dragons! Come!>

I stole a furtive look up the canyon walls where the men crouched in alertness. How long before they grew impatient? How long would they wait before they—what *would* they do? Would they laugh at me? Would they shun me? Would the king send me home in disgrace?

At once my dragonfear shrank; I felt bold as a bear.

"Dragons, come!" I shouted aloud.

Silence.

I tried picturing a dragon in my mind as I called.

No dragons came.

I tried holding Skava aloft, tried calling the dragons *through* her, tried drawing a dragon in the snow.

No dragons came.

I stood on that river for the greater part of the day, calling aloud and calling silently, pleading with Skava to commune with them, as falcons are reputed to do. I drew more dragons in the snow, and even did a dragon dance, using my arms as wings and causing Skava to break out of her trance and bate and squawk. Though the dance was more for warmth than for calling. For it was bitterly cold. Cold wicked up from the ice through the bottoms of my feet; it numbed my legs and iced my veins. I had to move to warm my blood.

Twice in that long day the king called me back up to him. The first time, at the day's height, he invited me to warm myself at the fire beside him. He set food and brew before me, then asked if I had seen or felt anything of dragons. It was too painful to meet his expectant eyes or those of the hearth companions who surrounded him. I studied my dried fish and said that I had not. My glance slipped sideways to Kazan, and I thought I saw him look at me with pity—*pity*! I did not want his pity, and yet . . . I was in some strange way glad of it.

The king said nothing at first. I guessed he was trying to swallow his disappointment before his men. Then, "Well, the day is yet young," he said. "Try again."

The second time came much later, when the sun stains were vibrant in the sky. Now there was a palpable restlessness in the cliffside encampment. I heard men quarreling and dogs fighting before I was halfway up the slope. A pack of warriors converged about us as Orrik motioned me to the fire and brought me food and brew. Rog stood near Orrik—aggressively near—as the king asked me again if I had heard or felt anything.

I had to say that I had not, save for Skava's odd demeanor.

"She has had her chance, now, Orrik!" Rog cried. "We have squatted beneath this miserable ledge all day, freezing our flesh and cramping our bones. I say we go forth at once and flush out the vipers with shield-clashing!" There was a murmur from the assembled men, but the king cut them off.

104

"You have agreed to give her the span of a day and a night. And it is well known that dragons venture out oftenest in the deepest night. Would you break your word?"

"I am not an oath breaker, brother. But I deemed you would repent your folly by now."

"It is not folly!" Orrik bellowed. He looked at me, seemed about to ask me something, but then abruptly sent me forth again.

Now I had no heart for drawing or dances or anything but a tired and constant <come come come come come>. I nearly wished the king would call me up to him and proclaim my disgrace so I would no longer have to pretend. Twilight lingered faintly in the southern sky. The ice moon, now full, spilled its silver brightness across the snow, casting all into sharp relief. The encampment was a dark, narrow gash. From time to time a shout or the yip of a dog betrayed the presence of life. The birds had all gone by now; even they ignored my calls.

The cold numbed me and sapped my strength.

At times I thought I sensed the thrum of something deeper than my ears could hear, but I deemed it was only my mind, muddled from cold and tiredness and straining.

"I need not have feared those dragons," I said to Skava. "This is worse."

Skava did not respond but only kept gazing up the canyon.

I tried to keep my mind upon summoning the dragons, calling <come come come come come>, but my thoughts began to wander more and more, and odd bits of memory drifted in among the summoning.

<Come come come.>

Snuggled between my mother and my father, playing bone-pegs on the bed.

<Come come come.>

The doll my grandmother gave me, with the face of a wizened apple and a blue-embroidered gown.

<Come come come.>

The time when I was ill, and all the voices around me blurred and retreated beneath the thrumming . . . the thrumming . . .

<Come come.>

The dragon . . . what was her name?

Flagra.

The name rolled around inside my mind: the word my mother said that I had called in my sleep. A dragon's name.

<Come . . . Flagra.>

And there was a lightning bolt inside my head, fast and bright and blinding.

A rushing noise grew in the distance; I could hear it stirring in the branches of the stunted trees above the canyon, and then it was upon me, chilling my face, whuffling in my ears.

All at once a raven shot past me, skimming just above my head. Then the sky was full of birds, far more birds than before. They chirped, cawed, screeched, whizzed past me—not slow and lazy, but frenzied, as if they had gone mad. And beyond them, something glinted in the sky.

Skava gave a cry, bated off my wrist, and kept on pumping her wings. It took all my strength to grip her jesses, to hold her against the wind. Why had I not tethered her to her leash!

She lunged away from me, and I felt her jesses slip from between my fingers; she broke away; she was ringing up and up to join the whirlwind of birds.

"Skava!" I called, running after her. <Come!>

And then I saw it again, the thing beyond her in the sky.

It glittered in the moonlight. Wings. It had wings—but like no bird I had ever seen. It was longer, more fluid. And faster. It came faster, growing huger and even huger.

At last I found my voice, which had been cowering at the back of my throat.

"It comes!" I shouted. "It comes!"

Chapter 13

And dragons, being the most ancient of all creatures, hold by the old way of speech: Say little; convey much.

—THE BOK OF DRAGON

There was a deep, sharp, ripping noise in the air, growing louder and louder as if the sky were being rent apart. The dragon was growing, bearing down on me. It twisted through the black strip of sky, glinting green in the moonlight, trailing wind spouts that rustled in the trees and loosed showers of clattering rocks down the sides of the canyon.

I heard shouting in the encampment; beneath the ledge I saw a churning of movement pricked by quicksilver flashes of moonlight on metal. The king had sworn to protect me, but now I did not see how he could. Not with the dragon coming so fast. Not with the dragon so *big*, and the men so tiny.

I tried to root myself to the river where I stood because that was the plan: I would stay and call the dragon to me, and the men would shoot it down. But the dragon sped closer, loomed larger, until it filled the sky between the canyon walls: a massive, winged eel. And the panic grew and grew and then erupted inside me, and my legs were running, slipping, stumbling up the slope toward the encampment, and I didn't know how they had begun. I looked back over my shoulder. The dragon was *above* the canyon—too high for the men to shoot it—almost overhead.

The rushing, ripping-air sound filled my ears, and I breathed in an alien scent: like sulfur, like hot metal. I threw myself down, covering my head and waited for . . . what? A blast of fire? A raking of claws?

I heard it pass above: a whooshing wingbeat, and then a wind-wake roaring in my ears. When I looked up, the dragon was soaring far down the canyon. It crested a rise, then was hidden from view.

Slowly, I clambered to my feet. The world was still, save for the crying of birds and a faint distant thunder that might have been only an echo in my mind. A sprinkling of arrows littered the slope; I had not heard them loosed. My bearskin lay where I had dropped it on the frozen river.

The dragon was nowhere in sight. I looked up into the sky at the circling birds and thought I saw Skava among them but could not be sure. <Come,> I called. <Skava, come.> I strained to reach her with my mind but felt only restlessness, confusion.

Then a shout from the encampment.

"Kara!" Orrik's voice echoed off the canyon walls. "Call again!"

Again?

Was he *mad?*

I had called and it had come and the men had loosed their

109

arrows and nothing had stopped the dragon from killing me, save for its own wild reasons, whatever those had been. And now he wanted me to call . . . *again*?

"I . . . can't!" I held out my arms in a shrugging motion and started up for the encampment.

"Call!" the king shouted.

I kept climbing up the slope, pretending not to hear.

There was a commotion in the encampment; then something glanced off a rock to one side of me, sending up a shower of snow.

An arrow.

I stared at it, appalled.

Was he *shooting* at me?

No, he hadn't aimed for me. But he was warning me. He was telling me most forcefully not to come back up.

I wheeled around and ran toward the river, fighting back tears. He was leaving me here alone; he would *make* me face the dragon, even when he knew he could not protect me from it.

I would not call again. I would pretend to call until morning, and then Rog could begin with his shield-beating. I cared not if they held me disgraced.

I was still running when I felt it, a gust of wind that warmed my back. And a sound—I heard it now—like the breathing of the sky. And a smell—the hot-metal smell. My scalp went tight and prickly; the hairs on my neck stood on end.

I slowed, stopped, turned warily around.

It was the dragon.

Caught full in the glow of the moon, it hovered above the cliff, rowing gently with its wings. I stood transfixed, knowing that the king and his men could not see it; its head was above the ledge. It exhaled and a cloud of steam arose, veiling it in a luminous white mist. But through rents in the mist I clearly saw the green expanse of scales—and the fierce green eyes that looked down at me.

I stood stock-still, unable to move, to speak, to wave, to scream.

The dragon's wings pulsed against the sky—not hard and leathery like the wings of bats—but shimmery, light, as if fashioned from spider-spin. The breath-mist dispersed, and I saw that this dragon was huge, even bigger than it had seemed flying past. Its head alone was as tall as a man standing.

A twist of water trickled down from the ledge. Melting. The dragon's breath was melting the snow. Someone called out to me; I realized how I must look to them, standing here, agape.

I tried to shout, but my voice had frozen in my throat.

And a word blew into my mind, blew as a fire does, fierce and crackling hot: <Kara.>

And an answering word formed in my mind: <Flagra.>

And I was surprised and yet not surprised to find that I *knew* this dragon; I had known her long ago. I stared into her long green eyes, and she stared back into mine. A wave of memory rushed through me: a cool, dark place, and a comforting presence. Breath-warmth, a thrumming vibration, and milk—sweeter and thicker than goat's milk or cow's milk.

I moved toward her. <Flagra.>

So they were true, the tales they told of me and dragons.

Or just one dragon, I thought. Just this one: Flagra.

A chunk of snow broke loose, slid down the ledge, and skittered down the slope. And above it . . . a cluster of dark figures crouched at the very top of the cliff, near the dragon. They were carrying bows. . . .

<Fly! Flagra, fly!>

There was a clashing of sword on shield; Flagra whipped her head around to look, and the arrows sped toward her. Three dark needlepricks dotted her throat, bloomed into a spreading red smear.

There came a roar like a thunderclap, a painful roar that came in through my ears and caromed off the insides of my skull. Flagra lurched forward and down, vomiting flame into the encampment. Through the roar in my head I heard screams, and then a shouted command:

"Loose!"

A humming swarm of arrows flew toward Flagra's throat; they struck with a volley of soft, popping thuds. She roared again, and a blinding bright pain erupted inside my skull. I clasped my head in my hands, but the pain did not abate. I couldn't see; I couldn't think; all I knew was pain . . . until faintly in the distance beyond the pain I heard the echo of a roar and birds screaming and people shouting and then something huge was tumbling down the canyon—tumbling toward me.

Flagra.

I ran hard across the river, still half blinded by the light behind my eyes and the raw burning brightness of pain. Behind me: crashing noises, a whoosh of flame. I flung myself past the far riverbank, up the hillside—scrambling, stumbling, crawling—then turned around to look.

Flagra plunged down the opposite slope, peeled back the snow like a layer of skin and stained it with her blood, setting off a clattering avalanche of rocks and loose boulders. She bounced onto the river ice, which groaned, then creaked, then gave way with a deep, booming *crack*! The air filled with a hissing roar that drowned out even the screams of the birds. Great plumes of steam churned up from the river.

It was full of dragon.

<Flagra!> I called, but I knew that she was dead; I felt nothing in my head but pain.

I retched and vomited in the snow.

And then again: the ripping noise, the noise from in the sky. I looked up and saw them, two glimmering *things* flying low through the canyon.

Dragons.

I stood held by them; I couldn't move. Now I could make out the shapes of their wings; now I could see the twin flashes of their eyes. They were *not* coming for me, I saw. They were headed straight down into the canyon. Straight for Flagra. Straight into the range of the archers. Up in the cliffside camp I saw movement—glinting pricks of light.

The men had seen them.

Suddenly, I couldn't bear for it to happen again.

I stood, summoned up all my concentration and bent it upon the dragons. <Flee! Go away!>

There was a crackling brightness in my mind so quick I would have doubted I had felt it, had I not felt it before with Flagra. The dragons hurtled forward; they were almost in line with the archers; it was late, too late . . .

<Flee!>

And they banked up sharply, skimming the canyon walls. A flurry of arrows spewed out from the encampment, but the dragons were nowhere in sight.

Had they gone?

There was a moment of hush, when I heard only the cries of the circling birds and the retreating roar of dragonwind in distant trees. The moon hung low, like a pearl caught between the canyon walls. So quiet and so still—save for the birds. So beautiful—save for the track of the falling dragon, which gaped like a bloody wound in the snow, and the steaming puddle of blood near the river. Through rifts in the steam, Flagra's body loomed, a gleaming, coiled hillock. I could not see her head; it was shrouded too densely in mist.

A cheer went up from the encampment. Men swarmed down the slopes, slipping through the bloodied snow, brandishing knives for the trophy-taking.

And a great, aching sadness welled up inside me. I stumbled down toward Flagra, not knowing what I would do when I reached her.

Then Kazan was at my side. "Kara," he said, and his face was full of worry. He tried to steer me away from Flagra, but I shook my head and stumbled toward the clot of men around the dragon.

They opened up before me as they had done in the high hall that day, only this time not at all grudgingly. Then Orrik was there, flushed, jubilant. He grabbed me by the waist, hoisted me into the air, set me down again. "We've done it, Kara!" he said. "I knew we could!"

I tried to answer, tried to tell him that it was wrong, what we had done, but he ran roughshod over my words. "We've got the biggest one now, I think. They said a green was biggest, and this one is so much bigger than the others, it must be the one. I'll carve out the heart and start the bloodletting while the men take their trophy scales, and then we'll move to another place to call the rest of the beasts. They must have turned back when they saw the green one lying here. But you can call them on the morrow . . ."

In some corner of my mind I grasped that he did not

know I'd sent the other two dragons away. "But, your grace," I said, "I—" The king went on, not heeding me. I felt weak, light-headed, as if I had not eaten for days. Orrik said nothing about the danger I had been in, nor his failure to protect me, nor the arrow . . .

The dragon stench filled my throat—a thick, clotting, sulfurous smell, mingled with the reek of charred flesh. A wind gust tore open a patch of steam near the river and stripped bare a dragon eye: enormous, unseeing, glazed with a thin filigree of ice.

My knees buckled beneath me; I crumpled to the ground and blackness rushed in.

Chapter 14

A dragon's head, mounted, protects the hall from fire;
a dragon's heart, roasted, fends off the bite of blade;
a dragon's blood, boiled, repels the creeping death.

—THE BOK OF DRAGON

When I awoke I was lying in the dark, wrapped in furs. My insides felt hollow, wasted, like a tree with the heartwood burnt out of it. A fire crackled nearby; one side of me felt hot. Sounds of a distant commotion reached my ears: shouting and talking and a sporadic clanging of metal. Then came another sound: a familiar burbling. Skava!

I sat up quickly, and regretted it at once. My head felt as if something heavy had come loose inside it. I moaned and lay down again. But Skava was there, tethered to the tree root in the cliffside encampment. The same place she'd been— when was it? How long ago?

I turned my head so that I could see her again, and my glance caught on the knot that leashed her to the root. Something amiss with it—it looped the wrong way. "Skava," I murmured. "What happened?"

For something had happened; I knew that. A chunk of memory broke loose. Calling. And Skava gone.

But she was here now. Back in the cliffside encampment. The fire . . . something about fire . . .

Dragons.

And more memories broke loose: the calling on the frozen river, the king's argument with Rog.

Flagra.

And I *remembered* her now, remembered from the time when I was small and had stayed in that dragon cave. Not whole, rounded memories, but just pieces: the gleam of Flagra's scales in the moonlight, the warmth of her sulfur-smelling breath, the sweet, thick taste of milk. And those eyes: long as my forearm, green as a jade stone. The *presence* of her flooded my mind as if I had never forgotten it—fierce, protective, more motherlike than dragonlike.

Flagra.

Had she spoken to me then? Is that how I'd known her name?

But she hadn't spoken to me this time, at least not in the usual way. I hadn't heard her name—I had *felt* it forming in my mind.

And how came she *here*? Before she had been south of here, near my father's steading.

Talking. Someone was talking. Two people, arguing in soft voices behind me. Something about the king, one of them said, and the other, "Let her rest," and then an answering retort and retreating footfalls.

I sat up again—slowly, this time—and twisted around

to look. There, with firelight flickering across his face, sat Kazan.

"You're awake," he said.

I began to nod, but my head felt unstable, as if tipping it the slightest bit would hurt.

"Here," Kazan said and held out a hornful of brew. "Drink this."

The brew was sweet, of course. Too sweet. Still, it warmed me all the way down. I knew I had things to ask him, but my thoughts clattered around in my head and I couldn't catch just one. At last I seized upon something: the knot.

"Who tethered Skava?" I asked. "The knot is mistied."

Kazan raised his eyebrows incredulously. "You fainted dead away back there, and I feared you were injured or ill or worse . . . and now you complain about a *knot*?" He laughed and shook his head. "You Krags," he said, pouring more brew into my goblet, "are so—what is that word? Arrogant. You think you have the only way to do a thing."

"So *you* did it?"

"She was perching on a rock at the top of the canyon. I borrowed your lure, and she came to it."

"You . . . *lured* her?"

"You thought I know only how to snare a bird, and the finer arts elude me." It was a statement, not a question.

I shrugged.

"Well, I have talents you know nothing of," Kazan said. "You would be surprised if you knew me better."

He was grinning at me now in a way that warmed my insides, as his too-sweet brew had done. But something still tugged at my mind. Something amiss . . .

The sound came again, a metallic clanging from outside the encampment.

"What's that noise?" I asked.

"They're gutting the dragon," Kazan said. "They're cutting out its heart and its kidneys and draining its blood. And some of the men are still taking their trophy scales. . . ."

My stomach lurched—I almost lost the brew—and the rest of my memory flooded in on a rush of darkness: the archers, the blood, the roar, the pain. I turned away from Kazan, buried my face in my hands, tried to wall myself off from the nightmare.

Kazan was talking—something about sorry, something about water—but I could not attend him.

I had *felt* her die. I had kenned her thoughts. She was . . . sentient—no less than a woman or a man. She had saved me with her milk, that long-ago time, and for that I had called her to her death. The shame of it burned inside me.

"Kara!" The king's voice brought me up with a jolt. "They *said* you were awake!" Orrik climbed up into the encampment, his face flushed and jubilant. A gang of warriors crowded in behind him. "I was worried about you, Kara. You just *dropped* back there, and we feared . . . By the sun's blessed rays, I am glad to see you well! We're moving the camp upriver. The dragons came that way, and we scouted out a better place, hemmed in by cliffs on three sides. We'll attach our arrows to the fishnetting and loose it over them when they come to your call."

When they come to my call.

I must call . . . *again?*

I gaped at him, dumbstruck. How could he take this so lightly, so *joyfully?* After what I *did.* After Flagra . . .

119

"Your grace, she will need rest . . ." Kazan began.

"You—you *shot* at me!"

I hadn't meant to say it, but the anger boiled up inside me and the words were out before I thought.

Orrik's face blanched; he worked visibly to compose it. I felt the pressure of Kazan's hand laid on my shoulder—for reassurance or restraint, I knew not which.

"No, Kara," Orrik said at last, his voice smooth and unperturbed. "I would never shoot at you. Never. But I commanded you to stay, and you"—he paused deliberately—"did not hear. And so the arrow was . . . a signal."

A *signal*? That had been no signal! It had been a threat! There was no intent to hit me—that I knew. But to frighten me into doing his will—yes!

And now I saw the game he played. Much as he might wish to punish me for defying him, he would not. He dared not throw me over. For I was like the fabled goose that laid the golden egg, and my help was needful for his plans. So he would humor me and cajole me and flatter me. He would threaten only without seeming to threaten.

But I couldn't call more dragons to their deaths. *Couldn't.* If I told my true reasons, Orrik would not understand. He would *force* me to call. So I would try to persuade him by means he could grasp.

"My king," I said, "I know but one dragon name—Flagra—that my mother told me. I spoke this name in my sleep, from the time they left me for dead in that cave. And it was not until I said this name—called it—that the dragon came. And *she* was the one who came. Flagra. The one who nursed me back—" I choked up, fought against the tears that pushed against the insides of my eyes.

"You are tired," the king said. Cajoling me. "Fetch her fish and more brew!" he commanded.

"No!" I tried to stand, but the dizzying pain in my head returned, so I sat back down. "You mistake my meaning. I *can't* call any other dragons because I already called the one whose name I know. I know no other names."

"Three dragons came," the king said, his blue eyes steady on my face, "and you called but one name. Do you call *birds* by their names when they come?"

"No, but . . . birds are *birds*. With dragons it is different."

"I have heard that dragons hunt only at deepest night. Could not *this* be why they bided so long?"

He was condescending to me. He would not heed what I had to say.

"It may be true, your grace—what she says," Kazan protested.

"All *too* true," came another voice, a voice I well knew. Rog. I picked out his face from the crowd of warriors around the king. "It's a fluke that dragon was here. It's the only one she knows."

"Be quiet, Rog." The king's voice held a threat.

"Orrik, now is time for the shields. I can lead a band ahead; you can—"

"*Cease!*"

Rog backed down like a beaten dog. Something had happened up in the encampment, some shift in power, when the dragons had come down to me.

"Let me show you something, Kara." The king held out his hands and helped me to my feet. He supported me with his arm and led me to the edge of the cave; warriors yielded

121

before us and closed again around us, leaving Kazan neatly behind. My head still throbbed painfully; my eyes ached.

The ice moon lit the eerie scene below: an army of men moving about Flagra's long, twisted body, festooned with wisps of mist. She was chipped and gored and hacked at. Icicles dripped from her jaw and brow ridges; blue-white ice scabbed over her eyes.

The king was talking: about the blood feud and the famine and the dragons killing sheep. He spoke of duty and honor and the glory I would gain when the dragon kyn was slain.

His words washed over me. I stared down at Flagra and was flooded with a deep, still sadness.

This was wrong.

It would do me no good to protest further—I saw that now. Orrik was too much bent on his course and the glory it would bring him.

But glory meant nothing to me now.

"We leave in a while to set up camp in the new place," Orrik said. "It is well past deepest night now, and the dragons, if they are yet hunting, will soon return to their lair. We must hasten, for we will be two days stringing net to arrow and setting all in place. Not next night, but the following, you will call." He turned and eyed me sharply, as if daring me to argue.

I had no wish to argue. I desired only to flee, to run, to escape into the hills.

"I . . . you are right, of course, my king. I am tired . . . perhaps sleep will clear my mind." I turned my face up toward him and gave him what I hoped was a brave-looking smile.

"That's my girl," he said, softening, and chucked me lightly under the chin.

* * *

We left early the next morning, a quiet, torchless caravan across the moonlit valley. Orrik offered to let me ride on the dogsled, but I would not, for it also bore Flagra's head and her heart and pig bladders full of her blood.

I skied along slowly in the company of Kazan and a friend of his, Thowain, who was a favorite of the king. Kazan carried my pack; Thowain offered to carry Skava, but I shook my head no. Although she still seemed distant, even the weight of her on my fist was a comfort. I gently scratched her feet; she turned to me, burbled, then went back to staring upriver.

The other warriors—even the hearth companions—seemed to have changed toward me. One offered me a draught from his drinking horn; another proffered me his cowl; many nodded and smiled.

The way was not hard; we followed the frozen river up the canyon, the way the dragons had come. The pain in my head had eased; now it was only a weight against the insides of my eyes. I pretended to listen to what Kazan and Thowain said, but my mind was tired and numb; it seemed to trudge wearily among memories and plans for escape and the paralyzing dread of calling anew.

At last we left the river and turned aside into a narrow gorge run through by a frozen creek. The rock walls stood well apart where we entered the gorge but curved closer farther on, until they pinched together at last, severed only by a narrow cleft. We stopped and made camp near the end.

I was sitting by one of the campfires, feeding Skava on my fist, when all at once there came a flash of light back the way we had come, and the sky flared pinkish red. Skava

123

stretched herself up and looked about alertly. All stopped their talking and stared in silence.

"They came back for us," one man muttered darkly.

"No," another said, "I have heard they do this, set fire to their dead. It is nothing to do with us."

They spoke in low voices, although they could not have been heard from so far. But there was something about that place that made us not want to break the hush.

S leep came quickly when I retired to my tent. The past day's work had truly drained me. When I awoke, the sun had already come and gone. I stumbled outside my tent to find Kazan feeding Skava. "I knew she must be hungry," he said, "and I didn't want her to wake you."

I nodded, grateful for the sleep and yet a little jealous that Skava would consent to be fed by someone other than me. But she had come to Kazan the day before, and I was glad of that.

I retrieved my gauntlet from my tent and finished feeding her. My headache had gone. My thoughts came clearly now and hardened me in my resolve to escape.

It was yet quiet in the encampment. Some of the men slept; others ate or tended to their weapons or talked quietly among themselves. The purplish bruise of twilight spread across the southern sky, while dark clouds massed in the north. The air smelled of coming snow.

When I had done feeding both Skava and myself, I blocked her within my tent and made for the place where the walls of the gorge converged upon the frozen stream. I preferred to relieve myself out of sight of the encampment; the warriors were used to my habits now and did not question me as I clambered up the stream's frozen path through the cliffs. I dared not go too far; that would excite suspicion, which I could ill afford. And yet I did venture far enough to assure myself that the creek seemed not to drop from above but rather to wind in gradual steps through a gap it had cut in the cliff rocks. Later, when all were sleeping, I could follow its path up and over the shoulder of this peak—and make good my escape.

Chapter 15

Fortune hath more twists in it
than a hank of new-shorn fleece.

— KRAGISH

FOLK SAYING

When I returned to the encampment, the last purplish traces of twilight had faded above the southwestern fells. Clouds rolled in from the north, blotting out the stars, drifting like windblown veils across the full moon's face.

The men sat in clusters around scattered fires. Some oiled their bows and leather gear, others worked with the fishnetting; all conversed in lowered voices. Kazan rose and came to me. "Will you sit with us, Kara?" he asked. I nodded and followed him to a group of men gathered about one of the fires.

I bided there a time, drinking the brew the men offered me, eating the food they brought me. This they did one by one, as if by signal; when I had finished one draught, someone who had not yet offered appeared and filled my horn. I drank slowly and sloshed some of the brew over the edge, as I did not wish to blunt my alertness this night. Feigning interest in the dragon hunt, I asked Kazan to show me the knot by which arrow strings were attached to the netting. "I deemed *you* were the mistress of knots," he said and then grinned—a bit sadly, I thought—and showed me anyway.

It seemed to me that the dragons might simply burn their way out of the netting, and, when I said as much, they rushed to explain it to me—the king's plan. They would array themselves upon the cliffs, hauling up the netting, which they had attached by long strings to their arrows. As the dragons approached, the men would loose their arrows at once, and the netting would entrap the creatures.

"Like a flying snare," one man said.

"More to entangle them than to enclose them," added another.

"So long as their wings are pinned, it matters not if they breathe flame," put in a third. "We'll fill them full of iron."

You will *not*, I thought grimly but said nothing.

There were two nets, it seemed: one for the first wave of dragons and the second for any that came later. "And after, we will lie in wait for the ones who set fire to their dead," Thowain said.

Kazan had remained silent during this exchange. Thowain, who sat to one side of me, leaned in and said softly, "Kazan asked to stand by your side in the canyon, but the king said his presence might warn off the dragons." I flicked a glance at Kazan, but he did not look up from his knotting.

I stayed for a while, pretending to accede to this plan, not wanting to waken suspicion. At last I bade them all good night and rose to go to my tent. Kazan rose as well and walked with me.

The men were silent as we wended our way among the fires, but I felt their eyes upon me. Then a voice from somewhere behind called out: "Good fortune, Lady Kara." I stopped, turned around to see who had spoken, but then came another voice—"Good fortune, Lady Kara,"—and another and another, building to a crescendo of grave, quiet voices. The king's tent flap stirred; he came to stand in the opening as the men greeted me, as their voices trailed off into silence.

I stood still, overcome. A lump had risen in my throat; I could not trust myself to speak. At last I said, "And to you."

I turned around and walked the short remaining distance to my tent; Kazan went before me and lifted the flap. Our glances snagged again, and this time his dark eyes were unguarded—stripped bare of all formality, abrim with unspoken emotion. They pierced me through.

I nodded briefly, ducked my head, and stepped inside my tent. I sat still in the dark, drawing the cold air deep inside me and pushing it out again, waiting for my heartbeat to calm.

I would never see him again.

Food.
That was what mattered, I told myself. Not Kazan, nor any of the others.

Food.

All else stood in readiness. I had flint and iron and tinder. I had candles—three good tallow ones that Gudjen had packed for me—and a fur for sleeping in. I had a dagger, and rope for snares, and a bow and seven arrows. I had a store of mice for Skava. If it came to the worst, I could release her to hunt for herself. But I could not rely upon her to feed me, and my seven arrows would not go far.

I lacked food. Only food.

If I could keep to a straight course, westward to the sea, I would be three days walking, I judged. Barring storms and wolves and obstacles unforeseen. Our party had come farther in three days—an angled course, north and east—but our luck had been good, and the dogs had hauled our heaviest provisions, and we had not had to stop to set snares. I would make for Skogsby, a seacoast trading town north of Orrik's steading. I did not deceive myself that I would hit upon it straightly. Three days to the seacoast, another two or three to Skogsby.

With luck, that is. Good fortune.

But I could not rely on good fortune alone. I would need food for a septnight, at least.

What I would do when I came to Skogsby I did not know. I had gold—the rings on my neck and fingers—which I could trade for food and a cloak to disguise myself and ship passage. I would have to fit myself into the life of the town— find work of some kind, until the ships began sailing in spring.

And then home . . .

But my mind balked at straying too far into thoughts of home. Home would not be the same—this I knew.

I could not dwell on that now.

Food. I lacked only food.

I would have to steal it from the sled. There was no other means. I could not *ask* for a septnight's worth of food without arousing suspicion. I could not live off the land. Not in the dead of winter.

So I stayed inside my tent and tried to sleep—vain effort!—until the talking stilled and scattered rumbles of snoring met my ears.

Slowly, I opened my tent flap—only a crack. The looked-for snow had begun to fall. This was fortune that cut both ways. It would hide my tracks from my pursuers, but it would also hide the land and stars from me. It was easy to become lost in the snow. Even in familiar terrain.

But I knew how to make a snow cave and go to ground safely until the storm passed. If I could find wood. If I had food.

I looked for the dogsled in the dark and found it where I had known it would be, near the center of the encampment. The dogs slept quietly in trenches they had dug in the snow. Now to find the sentries. There would be four. Always there were four. Two I found quickly, near the king's tent, stamping their feet and swathed in furs. Another I spotted halfway round the edge of camp, to the left. The fourth I could not see.

I opened my tent flap and craned out to look the other way.

"Lady Kara?"

I nearly jumped out of my skin.

It was the fourth sentry; he was stationed by my tent.

So much for stealing; now to beg.

"What may I do for you, Lady?"

I put one finger to my lips, motioning him to silence. He was young, I saw. Perhaps younger than I. He was tall and plumpish and eager-faced.

"I am . . . hungry," I whispered.

"I'll go get—"

"Wait!" I clutched at his arm to stop him. "I lost one day's meat and missed another's. I could eat a whole ram."

He nodded. "I will bring plenty." He started to go again, but I did not release his arm.

"I will need some . . . for the morrow . . . when I call."

He hesitated, and I feared I had gone too far. But, "Three days' worth I will fetch you," he said, smiling.

I released his arm and watched through the gap in my tent flap. One of the king's sentries met him at the tent; they spoke in low voices, looking my way. Then the king's sentry returned to his post, seemingly satisfied.

When my sentry returned, he put into my arms a full hemp sack. I opened it.

Dried fish, a rock-hard hank of barley bread, strips of dried reindeer meat. Three days' worth this might be for a burly youth, but if I stinted I might stretch it to a septnight.

I looked up into his beaming face and felt a wave of shame. He was so eager to please, and I had played him false. But too late to go back now. I would need that food. "I am . . . truly grateful," I said.

I hoped he would not be too severely punished for his kindness.

I stuffed the food into my bulging pack, leaving out one small hunk of meat, then strapped on skis and sat down to wait until the sentries roused their replacements. Before long I heard footfalls moving past and then a low rumble of voices. I shouldered my pack, groaning inwardly at its weight. Then I took up Skava and peered out. The sentries—I counted eight of them—stood talking near the king's tent. I stole behind my own tent, then lobbed the hunk of meat at the sleeping dogs.

A yelp. A low, rolling growl. Then all fury broke loose: howling, yipping, snarling, shouting. Men converged upon the dogs from all about the camp. I set off at a fast shuffle for the frozen creek. Falling snow blurred the way before me. Behind, I heard the lash of a whip, sharp whining, a burst of shouting voices.

Had they seen me?

But no. The voices receded.

I schussed through the snow as fast as I could, but with the overloaded pack weighing me down and Skava on my fist I was awkward, unbalanced, and slow. I could barely make out the cleft in the rock wall. I turned back one last time to look at the encampment. Only shadows. Dancing shadows, softened by snowfall and smudged by the glow of smoldering campfires.

At last I reached the cleft. I took off my skis—hurrying, hurrying, fumbling,—then tucked them under one arm and stumbled up the snow-covered creek. The cliff walls closed in around me. I made my way round a bend and then looked back.

Nothing. Nothing but rocks and dark and snow. The camp was out of sight. I held Skava close, put my face down near to her feathers, and breathed in the dusty-spice smell of her. I listened above the beating of my heart for the cries of alarm I knew would come.

A grumble of voices, fading to silence.

With a sigh of relief, I lashed my skis to my pack and began my ascent up the frozen creek.

It grew narrower as I walked. I dared not think what would pass if the creek grew so narrow that it closed up entirely. I would cope with that when I came to it. It was so dark and the snow came so thickly that I could scarce see the way ahead—only an arm's length or two. I *felt* my way up that creek, sometimes sinking knee-deep in drifts, other times clambering over boulders stripped bare of all but the new-fallen snow.

And always I strained my ears, expecting to hear shouts of alarm behind.

A strange, glad feeling began to fill me as I groped my way up the stream bed. I hardly marked the leaden weight of my pack or the fine-grained snow that pelted against my face. I had escaped the king's men. They had not followed, nor were they likely to track me if this snow kept up. "We did it, Skava," I said. She darted a glance at me, as if to acknowledge my words, then turned forward again. I could feel her excitement, twin to mine.

And so the shout behind me took me by surprise.

"Kara!"

I stood stunned for a moment, my bloodbeat hammering in my ears. Then I pressed forward up the creek as fast as I could, half walking, half trotting.

They knew. They were following.

My feet faltered and slid; my pack jounced heavily on my back. The creek had pinched in nearly to nothing. But I rounded a bend and a way opened up on my left: a hummocky incline that reached to the top of the ridge. A rock slide, it must have been.

Hurry!

I picked my way up the slope as fast as I could, but carefully, carefully. These rock slides were perilous to climb when the ground was not frozen solid. Gravel shifted beneath my feet, but otherwise the slope held firm.

When I reached the crest, I looked down where I had come.

Shadows. Only shadows.

The snow had nearly stopped; the moon, bounded by ragged clouds, blued the snowfields that stretched out beyond. I was standing on the shoulder of a great hunched hill. Or perhaps it was a mountain. It seemed high as a mountain, though not so steep.

Should I go over? Or down and around?

Then I heard it again. The voice. My name.

It seemed to be but one man calling. A thought struck me. Might it be Kazan . . . coming to help?

I hesitated, listening.

Nothing.

I thrust upward and to my left, skirting a hollow in the side of the mountain.

There was a crunch of shifting rocks; the ground slid beneath my feet. A clattering sound. A *whump!* of collapsing snow. My heart pitched up into my throat, and I was falling, down and down.

Chapter 16

With dragons it is as with birds:
males wear the brighter plumage.

—THE BOK OF DRAGON

My feet hit first, but my legs buckled and I came down hard on one hip. I lay clutching Skava's jesses as she bated, while the last clattering rivulets of rock played themselves out.

Black. All black. I could hear the beating of Skava's wings; I could feel, against my cheek, the breeze they stirred. But I couldn't see her, anymore than if my eyes had been shut tight. I could see nothing—not even my own hand before my face.

Her wingbeat stopped. I groped for her, found her, settled her upon my fist. "Are you all right?" I asked. My voice made an echoey sound. She seemed well enough by the feel of her, but I could not know for certain.

I wiggled my toes, moved my legs and arms, twisted side to side. The bottoms of my feet throbbed, one arm ached, and my hip felt sore where I had landed on it. But nothing worse.

I reached out my arm and tried to *feel* this place where I had fallen. There was a damp smell to it. Beyond, in the blackness, I heard the *plink* of dripping water.

A cave. It must be a cave.

My hand met with nothing save for the cushion of mixed snow and gravel beneath me.

I must have dropped through the roof of it. But then . . . why was it utterly black? Surely there would be moonlight. . . .

Unless the snow had sealed it up.

All at once the air felt smothery, hard to breathe.

Frightened, I shrugged off my pack, switching Skava from one wrist to the other, and fumbled about for flint and iron and punk and a candle.

Broken. All the candles felt broken. I collected the pieces, groped about for my dagger, severed the linking wicks.

I couldn't strike fire with Skava on my wrist, so I perched her on one knee and tethered her jesses to my sash. The spark was struck at last, and when I had lighted my stub of candle I looked about me.

Massive cones of dripstone pended down like icicles from the ceiling and sprouted up from the floor, as if we sat between the jaws of some many-toothed beast. I held up the candle to see whence I had fallen. There was an open shaft up through the rock, but no light shone in.

Well, I had lost my pursuer, at any pass. Whoever it had been.

It was silent—utterly silent—save for the *plink* of dripping water. The air smelled stale and never stirred.

We were trapped.

Still, this cave was big, I saw, as I moved my candle about. Far too big to smother in.

My breathing eased. "There *must* be another way out," I murmured to Skava.

I took her to fist—she looked unharmed—and walked among the dripstone. It was damp and slimy to the touch, and seemed to be coated with something white. In some places the ceiling dripstone had joined with the floor dripstone, forming pale, knobby pillars. And here—a narrow tunnel. Leading where?

I returned for my pack and skis; one ski was cracked, but not beyond repair. The candles and fire tools I rolled into my sash, then slung the rest over my back again and made for the tunnel. It soon converged with other passages—some close and winding, some so low-ceilinged that I had to crouch, some wide as a man is long, and twice as high. There were times when a passage narrowed down too tightly to admit me; then I retraced my steps and returned back the way I had come.

Of caverns there were many. Some were smaller than a bedcloset; others more spacious than Orrik's high hall. In the flickering light of my candle, I saw crystalline springs that glittered like frost; I saw ceilings festooned with dripstone; I saw walls like rippling curtains of pink and yellow and gray. And all around echoed the sounds of dripping water and runneling streams.

At first I counted caverns and tried to fix them in memory, but after a time they began to merge together in my mind. I began marking the walls with smoke to discover if I only wandered round in circles. But there *must* be a way out. These passages could not just wind about inside the bowels of the mountain and never find their way to air.

Skava, I marked, had returned to her old staring and seemed to face in one direction only, no matter how I turned.

"What do you hear?" I asked her.

And then *I* began to hear it—or imagine that I did. Strange, echoing noises. Distant rumbles and thumps.

I recalled the stories I had heard of trolls mining silver and gold in the mountains.

Trolls. I clung to the thought of trolls because I did not truly believe in them—while another, more likely surmise crept into my mind.

Dragons.

Could *they* lair here, in these very caverns? Was that why Skava seemed intent?

No matter. Must get out of this place. Must push my way through the dank, suffocating darkness and into fresh air.

I had carefully minded my pieces of candle, burning each down as far as possible, then lighting a new piece from the old. Now the stub I held burned low; I reached into my sash for another. There. I found one. But . . . only one. The last.

And my fear came rushing in: fear of the dark; fear that I was lost; fear that I would die here, and never a soul would find my bones.

Skava fluffed her wings. She leaned down and nibbled at my glove, then burbled at me. And somehow, that calmed me.

"We *will* get out of this place," I told her grimly.

The bumpings and rumblings grew louder. I moved toward them, for whatever came into this place must also have means of going out. Still, it was hard to tell whence they came, for sound echoed confusingly.

I watched where Skava faced and bore in that direction when I could. For I feared being lost in this cave more than coming upon the dragons. There were but five of them, Orrik had said—now four. And they went out to hunt at deepest night. So if there *were* dragons here, surely I could hide until they left to hunt, and then escape out the mouth of their cave.

A muted, echoing crash.

A rushing, rumbling sound, like a bonfire.

The passage climbed steeply; light faintly limned the edge of the wall where it curved up ahead. Rounding the bend, I could *see* ahead of me, beyond my candle's glow.

Moonlight.

The flame flickered, stirred by a breeze.

Fresh air.

I came to a halt and took thought.

I was safe in the passage where I stood. It would admit nothing so large as a dragon. I blew out the stub of my last candle and enfolded it in my sash; I could see well enough without it.

A sudden commotion erupted ahead of me, like the sound of water falling. Then a low, rushing, crackling noise: distant, reverberant with echoes.

Fire?

Dragonfire?

I could stay here—listen and wait. I ought to do so.

And yet . . .

I ached to know for certain. If these were dragons. If there were truly a way out.

Warily, I moved forward. The passage sloped up, widening, brightening. The sounds came clearer now: water and fire and the scrape of something on sand. There was a sporadic rumbling whoosh, like the sound of the sea within a coiled shell. And a strange, low murmuring that I seemed to feel rather than hear. The air moved: thin, chilly currents and floating drifts of warmth. A whiff of something . . . something burning . . . sulfur . . .

Another bend in the passage. I crept around it; the passage ended and gave onto a broad rock ledge. Beyond, the floor dropped away sheer into a cavern. From where I stood I could see only the roof of it—dripping with stone icicles, awash in light.

I ventured onto the ledge, first crouching, then dropping to hands and knees. Or rather *hand* and knees, for I held Skava aloft on my left fist. When I had nearly reached the edge, I lay on my stomach, scooted the last remaining distance, and peered down into the cavern.

I drew in a sharp breath.

It was a vast chamber—larger than any great hall—larger than a score of great halls put together. At one end a huge opening gaped in the rocky wall, and beyond, I saw what I had hoped for: the snowfields, bright with reflected moonlight.

And below, as I had known, were dragons.

But not only four of them. There were ten times that, at least. Dragons slumbered in great glittering heaps all about the chamber floor. Those just below me looked large as knolls. Farther back, they seemed to shrink to the size of mice, though I knew it was only the vastness of the cave that made them seem so.

Some few dragons seemed to be flying—no, not flying—liker to *floating* in the air below. These floating dragons looked smaller than the others, though each—I saw by the near ones—was larger than any horse. One flamed suddenly, dropping down lower, then gradually rose again through drifting tendrils of smoke. They seemed to be sleeping, or resting, or idling away their time.

Skava made a soft, anxious sound in the back of her throat. "Shh!" I said.

One of the smaller, floating dragons jostled against a stone icicle near the bottom of the cave; the dripstone crashed to the ground, shattering, clattering, echoing against the walls. A big green dragon opened its eyes and shot out a warning lick of blue flame. The smaller dragon twisted quickly away, then plunged into the pool in the center of the cavern, sending up a curtain of sparkling droplets. Another floating dragon flamed; the water evaporated into a hissing blue veil of mist.

These were children. They *must* be children, and they seemed all of an age. Some were red and others green, just as with the older dragons. The younger ones were brighter in hue; some of their elders were so dark-hued as to be almost black. And I knew, without knowing *how* I knew, that the red ones were male and the green, female.

I could not tear away my gaze. These dragons minded me of the whales I had seen disporting along the seacoast—huge, silent, joyous. This place—the dragons, the mist, the echoes, the suffusing blue light of the moon—seemed touched by a strange enchantment. So intently did I watch that I did not mark the floating dragon until too late. He wafted up from below me, from under the ledge; by the time I could recover from the shock, we were nearly face to face.

I screamed. Skava squawked and bated off my fist. The dragon gave a start, belched out a jet of flame. I scooted backward, blinded by the stinging smoke, holding my left arm straight out with Skava bating from it. I scrambled to my feet, turned around to go back to the passage—and then drew up short.

I was staring into the eyes of the selfsame dragon; he had alit upon the ledge behind me and now stood blocking my way.

He cocked his head, as if curious. "Hush, Skava," I murmured. She calmed; I settled her back on my fist. I feinted right, then tried to slip to the left and past him. He thrust out a talon, blocking me.

And a prickling sensation ran up the back of my neck. Something behind me . . . Slowly, I turned around and peered down into the cavern.

Eyes. At least forty pairs of them. Long and green and slotted. Dragon eyes—staring up at me.

Chapter 17

Dragons shun all prey that kens them.

—The Bok of Dragon

I stood rooted, caught between the multitude of staring dragons and the one that blocked my way.

Back. I must get back. Back into the passage whence I had come—too narrow for dragons to follow.

I wrenched my gaze from the dragons below and fixed on the one before me. He was taller than any man, this dragon. His long, thin neck curved down so that he faced me eye to eye. Green eyes he had, with long black slots: fierce beneath protruding ridges. All else was red—soft and chalky on his underbelly, brighter than fresh blood on his gleaming scales. His wings, red-veined, delicate as spider-spin, rippled at his sides.

There was room, I saw, to my right, where I might slip between wing and wall. Slowly, I edged forward.

The dragon's nostrils flared; his belly swelled with an intake of breath. He spat out a lick of flame.

I jumped back. Skava scolded the dragon with high, angry screams, struck at him with a foot. I coughed from the smoke, which smelled of burning wool.

The dragon's eyes glittered.

Did he laugh?

Now he sucked in another breath. I flung myself back. Flame splashed on the rock where my feet had been; Skava hissed but did not bate.

Was he toying with me, as a cat toys with a mouse?

Another breath. He was going to flame. I glanced behind me; I had nowhere left to go.

"Stop!" I said. My voice rang against the cave walls, then ebbed in rippling echoes.

The dragon hiccoughed, seemed to swallow his flame in startlement. A blast of smoke escaped through his nostrils; I coughed and edged to one side, astonished that my words had had effect.

There was a murmur below, a low, deep, pulsating thrum that seemed to drift through the throng of them and rumble in my bones. A green-black dragon—one of the largest—was uncoiling herself, was rising to her feet in a slow, fluid motion until she stood tall as a ship's mast, though still well below. Then others likewise rose, and now *all* of them were standing, contemplating me.

<*What* did you say?>

The words burned themselves into my mind and reverberated painfully against the inside of my skull. I clenched against the hurting until it ebbed to a pulsing throb.

The green-black dragon. She had spoken to me.

I answered—not aloud, but silently, deliberately, pur-

144

posefully, as if I had known how to talk to dragons for all my life: <I told him to stop.>

The murmur rose again, and this time I discerned the feeling of it—a feeling of wonderment. And I thought I picked out a word or two as well, though I could not be certain. *She speaks,* I thought I heard. Then the green-black dragon asked:

<Did *you* call Flagra?>

The words pierced my heart. *Flagra.*

<*Did* you?>

I looked down into the cavern, at the two-score pairs of dragon eyes staring up at me, and the shame of what I had done engulfed my fear.

<I did, but . . . I had no choice, they were forcing me to do it, and at any pass I did not recall her . . . it was so long ago . . .>

Silence. Mind-silence and ear-silence, with only the *plink* of dripping water to break it. My words seemed to hang feebly in the dank cave air, with all their cringing and weaseling and excuse-making clear to view. I wished I had stopped at *I did.*

<Give me your name.>

Her command blazed through my mind, left a raw, throbbing pain in its wake.

<Give me your name!>

<Kara!>

The murmur again. I felt my name drawn out of me, examined, commented upon like a piece of woven cloth from a faraway land, offered in trade by a merchant. A red dragon rose to its feet, seemed to say something to the green-black one.

The green-black one turned to me again. <So . . . *Kara.* You also warned two of our kyn of danger?>

A saving grace. I *had* done so. <Yes,> I said.

<Why?>

I felt the scope of this question contained within it and knew that nothing less than the whole and honest account of all my dealings with dragons would satisfy. Yet I knew not how to begin. <Because Flagra,> I faltered. <When I was young . . .> And then this, too, was drawn from me—the whole tale, beginning with my illness and my time in the dragon cave. It flowed wordless out of me in drifting shapes, like clouds that billow and twine and blend in the wind, until at last it thinned and dispersed.

And the dragons were looking at me in a way I could not fathom. Would they kill me now? I did not know. This was most strange, this silence. I had been taught that dragons were ravenous beasts, their hunger never restrained or sated. And yet here they stood, with me captive to them, *regarding* me with measuring eyes.

Then, <Loose the bird,> the green-black dragon said.

I blinked, startled.

<The falcon. Loose her.>

<You won't . . . harm her?>

<We hold no grudge against *her*. Loose her.>

I hesitated, wondering what that boded. Had the dragons forborne to harm me because of Skava?

<*Loose her.*>

Hastily, I freed Skava's jesses from her leash. She looked about her, roused, then sailed down into the cavern, alighting with a tinkle of bells upon the back of a big green dragon. Serenely, she began to preen.

Something seized me from behind. My pack straps yanked up hard under my arms; I was moving.

The floating dragon. He held me.

A scream escaped me as the ledge dropped away from

beneath my feet. The floor of the cavern swooped up. A jarring impact—my legs buckled, straightened—and I was standing in the cavern amidst the dragons.

They were immense.

They had seemed so from above, but now I felt as if I stood in a great dark forest with trees that glared and breathed.

Hot breath. Dry and metallic, like a forge.

I shrank back from the dragons' formidable feet: gnarled as tree roots, tipped by talons long as scythe blades.

The younger dragons—each taller than I and more massive than a bull full grown—moved toward me through the spaces between their elders. One brought her head down near me—so near that I could feel her warm, smoky breath, could see the mottled greens that patterned each particular scale. She nuzzled my stomach with her snout, then snuffled round to my pack. My food! She wanted my food. Then the other young ones began sniffing at me, poking, prodding, nudging. I did not sense that they wanted to harm me, but they were so big and their muzzles so hard that they hurt. I tried to back away from them, but they pressed me close on all sides; there was no room to move. Then a ripping noise—my pack! I whirled around, but then another snout poked me hard, and I fell backward onto the cave floor. They were crowding in nearer, breathing on me, a circle of curious, probing dragons when— *crack!*—lightning in my head.

The dragons turned as one toward the big green-black female, then slowly backed away from me. I had not understood the words—if words there had been—but the meaning was clear. They were not to harm me.

Not yet, at any pass.

The young dragons stared at me for a time, making low, grumbling noises. Then one flicked another with her tail, and still another shot flame at the tail-flicker. And they were off, cavorting in the pool at the center of the cave and playing what looked for all the world like a child's game of chase.

The older dragons settled back down, and a rumbling murmur arose from among them, so low that I could not tell for certain whether I sensed it with my ears or with my mind or only in the marrow of my bones. I strained to understand them but could not. Which was strange, I thought, since the green-black one's words to me had been blazingly clear.

I stood uncertainly, not knowing what to do.

Might it be . . . they would let me go?

I looked for Skava and found her still preening lackadaisically on the same green dragon she had flown to before. One of the dragon's back scales was notched—broken off, perhaps. I nearly called Skava but stopped, not wanting to draw notice. Anyway, I was irked at her. She had abandoned me readily enough.

I edged round the sleeping bulks of several dragons that lay between me and the cave mouth, skirting them widely, before I marked the dragon stretched across the mouth of the cave. Blocking it.

I took pause.

It did seem to be sleeping. And there was a gap between its tail and the cavern wall. Yet that tail . . . A ridge of crimson spines traversed it, sharp and jagged as shards of glass. I had just begun to sidle along the wall when the tail whipped in front of me and neatly closed the gap. I looked back at the dragon's head. One huge green eye surveyed me, as if I were not worth the effort of opening two.

I was a captive.

But why? What would they do to me?

I looked about to find a secure place to stand where I

would not be trodden underfoot. Near the pool, I saw, the broken-off roots of a cluster of dripstone icicles jutted up from the cavern floor. About forehead-high they stood—my forehead, not a dragon's. I worked my way through the cave to them, giving the dragons wide berth. Some few of the clustered stone columns had been broken off lower to the ground; gaining purchase on those, I climbed to the top.

When I looked down, all had changed.

The dragons were moving. I shrank back from them, but they did not come for me; they moved all around me and past me toward the mouth of the cave. Their wings rustled; their tails scraped against the sand; their breaths warmed me as they passed. Their gait was light—astonishingly light—lithe as a cat's.

A jingling sound: Skava streaked across the cavern and lit upon my shoulder. "So the traitor returns?" I said softly, scratching her feet. She stretched up and tweaked my hair. I considered seizing her jesses and taking her to fist but decided against it. The dragons seemed to . . . disapprove of my holding her captive—although they did not scruple to do the same with me.

They milled about at the mouth of the cave, where moonlight rippled like water across their great ridged backs.

The hunt, I thought. The nightly hunt.

They prodded one another, swished their tails. I heard a murmuring in my mind, and, though I could not separate out words, I felt the thrill of their exuberance.

Now one alone stood poised at the lip of the cave. She leaned slowly forward in utter silence . . . and disappeared.

I gasped, staring at the place where the dragon had stood. And then she reappeared in the air beyond, pumping up from below, her wings glinting with needlepricks of light. A cool draught of air gusted into the cavern. Another dragon launched itself, disappeared, pumped up into view—then another and another—a liquid tide of dragons flowing out of the cave and dwindling in the distant sky. There was a hush about them, which the whoosh of air beneath their wings seemed only to magnify.

Then the smaller ones took wing—quickly, clumsily, eagerly. They did not sink so far but seemed to bob on the air like hoarnut shells on a swift-flowing stream. They slipped side to side, stalled, dived one upon the other in what seemed like sheer joyous frolic.

And now Skava gave a cry, pushed off my shoulder, joined them in the sky.

<Skava,> I called, <come! *Come!*>

But she did not.

I watched until bird and dragons disappeared among the stars, and I was seized with a strange, wild longing to go with them, to cast off from this cave and *soar*.

But that was not to be. I was earthbound; they were free.

One dragon remained standing on the cave lip—the big dark red one. The guard dragon.

I stood watching, *willing* him to go so that I could escape.

He turned around, cast me a hard, glittering gaze, then stretched across the cave mouth and went to sleep.

Chapter 18

Clean your trencher.

—PARENTAL

ADMONITION,

KRAGLAND

It was quiet in the cave. The only sounds were the rumbling snores of the guard dragon and the echoing *plinks* of dripping water: round and musical where they dropped into the pool, flat and hard where they spattered on rock.

I had eaten a meal on my dripstone platform—eyeing the guard dragon all the while. But he had not so much as broken the rhythm of his snores. Still, I had no doubt that if I approached where he lay he would waken soon enough.

Now I looked about me for another passage out. The cavern was vast. Toward its mouth, it was silvered by moonlight—patching across the floor, glistening in the masses of dripstone high above. Farther back, all melted into shadow.

I could not possibly reach the passage I had entered by; the walls loomed too high, too sheer. But far back in the cave . . . who could know? I eased myself down the jagged steps to my platform and made my way across the sandy floor.

Movement flickered behind the watch dragon's eyelids, but they did not open.

I groped my way to the nearest wall and edged along it, running my hands across the cold, slimy surface, probing at every niche and hollow as high as I could reach.

It seemed a very long time that I felt my way in this wise, finding nothing but a crack or two for mice or voles to leave by. I had traversed but a small portion of the cave wall when I heard something—a faint, distant clanging from somewhere outside and below. Familiar somehow . . .

Shields! It was soldiers clashing swords against their shields! I stumbled to the front of the cave, as near to the watch dragon as I dared.

The clanging faded, trailed off. And a wave of loneliness engulfed me. I ached to see Rath and Myrra, to see Corwyn and the birds in the mews. Even Skava had abandoned me. And Kazan. I wondered . . . did he search for me? Was he sorry that I had gone?

Well, no matter about Kazan. I must get *out*.

I had just begun exploring the wall again when a soft jingling caught my ears.

Skava. She streaked through the cave mouth, grazed the watch dragon's back ridge. I held out my gloved hand and called her. She lighted down, burbled, then walked up my arm to perch on my shoulder. There was blood on her feet, I saw, and she had the fat, contented look of a bird that has eaten its fill.

"Your training is ruined," I scolded her. "Hunting on your own! I have plenty of mice to feed you." Calmly she ran her talons through her beak to clean them. I sighed, feigning vexation, but I knew I could not hide my gladness from her. "You're a traitor," I said, gently scratching her feet.

I had still found no passage when the first of the young dragons returned. There was a rush of air; I looked up in time to see the dragon tilt precariously to one side, right itself, teeter too far the other way. It belched flame, plummeted, and skidded onto the cave floor, flapping its wings and scrambling frantically for purchase, with all the grace of a duck landing on a frozen pond.

More young dragons came hard behind—tilting, flaming, dropping in a wild, ungainly commotion. Some brought prey with them—three or four rabbits I saw, and some ptarmigan, and a single gray fox. Each dragon with prey tore into it the moment it alit; the others crowded round, stealing bits and pieces as best they could.

I crouched beside the wall until the flow of dragons ceased, then quickly made my way back to the safety of the platform.

And just in time—for now the big ones came.

They soared into the cave one by one on thundering gusts of air—breathing out flame, trailing smoke—and then lit down with a fluid, sinuous ease that made them seem light as whiffle fluff. I crouched down low on my island, afraid that they would collide with it, but they never came near. Through the swirling smoke and the fine, choking dust I could make out their prey—large prey—a reindeer, an elk, a big buck ox. And yet most, so far as I could see, brought nothing.

Skava pushed off from my shoulder and alit on the back of a green dragon—her friend of the chipped ridge plate. The cave soon filled with a terrible, echoing cacophony of crunching bones and tearing flesh. It grew hot; the reek of blood mingled with the scorched, dragony smells of sulfur and smoke.

Yet there was an odd peacefulness about this feeding. I had thought that dragons would fight for prime morsels, as the sled dogs did. But these dragons did not fight. One yielded to another, or so it looked to me, save for the young ones, who wriggled in and out at will among their elders.

All at once, the dragons' heads jerked up. They stood as though listening, their eyes fixed on the cave mouth. Then I saw it too. Another dragon was flying toward the cave—plummeting sharply, lurching laboriously up again, wobbling from side to side. It skimmed over the watching dragons, hacked out flame with a plaintive mew, then thumped down, sprawling, at the foot of my island.

I felt a wail from one of the dragons; a murmur rippled among the others like a storm wind stirring the treetops. They crowded around the latecomer—a young red dragon—snuffling at it, poking it with their snouts. They loomed frighteningly near; I drew far back on my island. Still, the hurt one's cries pulled at me so, I could not help but watch.

Then a sudden hot blast blew into my mind: <Humans!>

And they were staring at me now—all of them—as they had not since they had first discovered me here.

I froze. What could this bode?

The wounded dragon cried piteously; my glance was drawn irresistibly down to it. And then I saw.

An arrow. It protruded from the dragon's side, below and just behind one wing. A dark red rivulet of blood welled up from the wound and ran down the dragon's belly.

I looked up with sudden fear into the eyes of the watching dragons.

<Humans!> The word whipped through my mind again as if it had been spat.

One of the larger dragons nuzzled about the arrow shaft, seemed to be trying to pull it out. The shaft snapped in two; the wounded one whimpered. Other dragons converged upon the arrow but only managed to bite the shaft down to a splintered nub.

They would never get it out. What they needed was . . . hands. Hands, and maybe a knife as well.

I rummaged in my pack until I found the dagger Gudjen had given me. Hesitating, I fingered its edge. How if I hurt the dragon, trying to help it? How if I *killed* it? I knew *I* would not live long past that. And yet . . .

The wounded dragon was whining with pain; it tore at my heart.

I drew in breath. "I think I can help," I said.

The big green-black dragon whipped her head up and spat a lick of flame in my direction.

<Go away,> she said.

<I have done this before,> I said, changing to the kenning way of speaking. <One of my brothers was shot in a hunt—>

The dragon shot me a look of pure scorn. <Go!>

<—and I dug the arrow out. With my hand.> I held up my hand and mimed pulling out the arrow. <And a knife.> I held up the dagger.

The murmur again, the rumbling murmur that rippled through them. I knew they were talking among themselves, but I could not separate out the words. At last, the big green dragon turned to me. I could see the pulse of her bloodbeat beneath her massive jaw.

<We watch,> she said.

I slipped the dagger into my sash and climbed down from my island. The dragons loomed all around me. I flinched at their every movement, for the slightest shift of foot or tail could crush me. A few moved reluctantly back to make room for me. The wounded one whimpered and whined.

And I recognized him now by his broad face and bright, wide-set eyes. He was the one who had blocked my way up on the ledge.

He seemed not quite as large now, lying down. The tallest point of him—his back ridge—came chest-high on me. I knelt by the wound and wiped my sweating hands on my cloak. Carefully, I placed my hands on the bloody flesh around the stump of the arrow shaft.

It had a thick, leathery feel to it, this dragon flesh. It was not hard and scaly like the dragon's back, nor thin and fluttery like its wings. This was the dragon's soft underbelly, and it felt—almost—like human flesh. Probing with my fingers, I could sense the hard lump of the arrow beneath the skin. I jiggled the shaft to discover how it lay; the dragon let out a sharp cry and clouted me with his wing.

I heard the shifting of dragons in the sand behind me; their hot breath stirred my hair.

I turned to the big green-black one. <I must hurt in order to help,> I said. <First, it will hurt.>

The dragon fixed me with her fierce slotted eyes. <We watch,> she said at last.

A bead of sweat trickled down the side of my face. I braced one foot on the wounded dragon's side near the shaft, then drew the dagger from my sash. Speaking to the green-black dragon, I said, <Now I must cut.> I slashed the air with the dagger.

The dragon eyed me long and hard. Then, <We watch.>

Any other time I would have cut slowly, carefully, sparing all the pain I could. But now I knew that if I were to cause

156

pain, I must have something to show for it—and soon. I grasped the shaft, readied the dagger, traced in my mind the line I must cut in the dragon's flesh. Then, holding my breath, I sliced down quickly and yanked hard on the shaft.

I sprang back at once, clutching the arrow.

The wounded dragon let out a howl that singed my hair; he beat on my head with his wing. The other dragons closed in around me, glaring. Their breath was hot—scorching hot. I held up the arrow. <Look!> I said quickly. <It's out!>

The dragons stared at the arrow, then turned back to the wounded one, who whimpered and moaned. At once they moved in close about him, shoving me aside, and began nuzzling him, licking his wound.

I scrambled up my dripstone island and huddled there, shaking.

Over the next few days I settled in to await my chance to escape. After what had passed with the arrow, I no longer feared so much for my life. The fierce contempt the dragons had held for me seemed to have softened to grudging toleration. They went about the business of their lives paying small heed to me, except when I drew too near to the cave mouth. Then one of them would warn me, by moving to block me or just *eyeing* me, that I was not to go out.

Meantime, I repaired my cracked ski with strips of leather cut from my sleeping fur. And at night, when the dragons left to hunt, I felt my way along the dripstone of the cavern wall, seeking a passage.

I marked my days by the hunt. It was the high point of the dragons' day, and it became so with me, as well. I came to love watching them poised at the lip of the cave, then dropping down and out of sight, then rising up through the dark mountains into the stars. Moonlight sparked off their scales; their wing-wind gusted in my ears. And all was hushed, as if they performed some ritual not to be tainted by the voicing of it. I was the only human ever to have witnessed . . . *this*.

During the second day I resumed my work with Skava, directing her to places ever farther afield: to the rocky outcrop just outside the cave mouth, to a needlecone tree below, to a crag across the gorge. On the fourth day I pictured the king's tent in my mind and tried to send her there. But she only looked at me, puzzled. I had not heard shield-clashing since that first night; likely they had all left by now.

Skava's progress seemed slower than it had used to be. She was wilder, more independent, less eager to please. But I resolved that one day, when she was ready, I would direct her to the mews—to Corwyn. And then I would summon them both back to me.

This work with Skava I did while the dragons slept, which they did for much of the day. Their sides rose and fell; their breaths escaped their nostrils in curling wisps of smoke. The younger dragons settled down in a clump: heads draped over tails draped over necks. Occasionally one would groan, or another would snort out a puff of smoke. Ofttimes they dreamed, their eyelids flickering, their tails twitching convulsively, like a cat immersed in visions of mouse-catching.

When they awoke, the young ones found their own diversions. Sometimes they played a sort of "catch." One dragon would puff itself up, curl into a ball, and hover in the air. Then the other dragons whacked it with their tails and sent it drifting slowly across the cave. Other times, they played the splash-and-flame game I had seen before. One dragon would plunge into the pool, sending up watery geysers; the other dragons flamed, vaporizing the geysers into fantastical phantoms of mist.

They minded me of Gudjen's steam-workings—her first with a single dragon and her second with many. She had presaged all, I thought: my calling of Flagra, this kyn of many dragons. And yet something felt amiss with the second steam-working; it did not ring true. . . .

The older dragons, upon waking, began a conversation that seemed to continue day to day. It rumbled through my mind, flowing from calm, droning murmurs to an agitated pitch, sometimes culminating in fitful exchanges of flame.

At first I could comprehend only snatches of meaning, as with some Ulian bondmaids we once had. I could understand them when they spoke only to me, but when they spoke among themselves, the words came so fast and overlapping that they seemed only gibberish. Still, as with the Ulians, the longer I listened to these dragons, the more I attuned myself to their speech, until I began to grasp the gist of it.

It was during these colloquies that I learned the dragons were hungry. Many had starved this past winter; they feared more would do so before long. For years the dragon kyn had been moving steadily north to escape the depredations of humans. But in these northern wastes, food was scarce. And still there were humans. Ever there were humans. Even the seas swarmed with their ships.

Some of the dragons wanted to move farther north to where humans were scarcer still. Others despised the cold, said the chill sapped their strength so they could neither hunt so long nor so far. And every night during the hunt two dragons went to seek out a better place to lair. They had found one cavern farther north, I gathered, but it was small and far from water, and whether or not to move there was a source of much contention.

Of me they said little. I learned only that they would not release me, lest I betray them to *my* kyn.

My own supply of food had dwindled alarmingly. By the sixth day I was down to two strips of elk meat and a hunk of barley bread, though I had stinted to stretch it out. Skava was not trained to hunt for me, and I could not teach her to do so unless I could go into the field with her, which the dragons would not allow.

Help came from an unexpected quarter.

It was after the hunt when the young arrow-struck dragon approached my island, carrying a rabbit haunch in his mouth. His wound had closed, I saw; it was only a dark, raised ridge on his side. I stood as he approached, backing away. He dropped the haunch at my feet.

<Eat,> he said.

Warily, I looked round at the other dragons. Absorbed in eating, they paid us no mind.

<Eat!> the red dragon insisted.

Gingerly, I picked up the haunch. It was bloody and raw and dirty. But I didn't want to offend him, nor provoke his wrath, nor discourage him from bringing more food. Besides, I was hungry.

Steeling myself, I took a bite.

<Good,> I said, chewing, pushing back my revulsion. I smiled brightly.

<It displeases you.> This, matter-of-factly; a statement, not a question.

<No, no, it's good but I . . .> There was no lying in

dragon speech, in which feelings count for more than words. I shrugged. <I like my meat cooked.>

<Cooked?>

<With fire. Flame,> I said.

The dragon regarded me speculatively. I lifted the haunch for another bite, and at that moment—*whomp!*—he belched out a blast of flame, setting fire to the meat.

"Yow!" I dropped the meat and jumped back from it, almost falling off my perch. The other dragons looked up sharply from their meat, and I heard a strange, low vibration that felt to me like . . . laughter.

I fanned the burning haunch with my cloak, the dragons watching me closely, until the flame went out. Then I picked it up, using a corner of my cloak to protect my fingers. I blew on the end of the haunch to cool it, and then I took a bite.

<*Good!*>

This time the dragon believed me. He slowly blinked his eyes; there was a gleam in them that I took for a smile.

He snorted out a burst of steam, then turned around and rejoined his friends.

Perhaps it was watching the young dragons play, with their fire and water and steam. Perhaps it was that my thoughts drifted more and more to Kazan. Or perhaps that the dragons' dilemma had begun to gnaw at the edges of my mind.

At any pass, an idea had begun to tease at me. I pushed it away at first. It was outlandish, unworkable. It trailed in its wake a dark, chilly current of fear.

But the idea kept nudging at me. At last, on the ninth day since I had come to the cave, I let it in.

Chapter 19

Power inhabits their names.

—THE BOK
OF DRAGON

I mulled over my idea for the better part of a day, pushing through the fear, persuading myself that I was only *thinking* about it and in no way beholden to act.

But in the end I knew that I must.

As long as there were dragons, the king's men would ever seek me. Nowhere would be safe—my father's steading least of all. And I could no more aid in the killing of these dragons than I could murder my own kin.

All my life I had run from things I did not want to do: to the hills to escape spinning, and even here to escape calling dragons. But now—if I were not to run for the rest of my life—I must make straight for the maelstrom's heart.

* * *

I bided until the early hours of the morning, until the dragons had returned from their hunt and had finished off their kills. The full-grown ones settled down to their rumbling colloquy, and the old contention arose again: whether to stay here or move farther north.

Shadows pooled around the dragons' massive forms. I could barely make out Skava, silhouetted on the back ridge of her favorite green dragon near the edge of the throng. I needed to speak to the big greenish-black dragon, but she lay somewhere in their midst.

I stood on my platform, waved to her.

Nothing.

<Dragon!> I called to her.

She paid me no mind.

"Uh, craving your pardon," I said aloud.

Not even a dimple of turbulence in the smooth rumble.

I cupped my hands around my mouth. "CRAVE PARDON!" I shouted, and my voice beat in dwindling ripples against the walls of the cave.

At once the rumbling stopped. A forest of dragon necks and heads swiveled round to regard me. Their eyes gleamed in the dark—wide, incredulous, outraged—as if a bondmaid had dared interrupt a parley of kings.

I found the big greenish-black one and spoke to her, not aloud, but in the kenning way. <I know a place,> I said. <It is far beyond the lands of humans, and it teems with prey, and it is warmed by a fire beneath the earth.>

There was silence in the cave, save for the echoing *plink* of dripping water. Even the young dragons had stopped in their play. Then a murmur slowly arose among the dragons: <A place, she knows a place? She? *She!*> The tone of it shifted from incredulity to indignation, and at last the green-black dragon's voice whipped through my mind: <What place is this?>

<An island, far into the northern sea. Whence Skava comes,> I said.

<If it is beyond the lands of humans, how came *you* to know of it?>

I related as best I could what Kazan had told me. Some of the dragons muttered skeptically about the absence of humans and the fire under the earth. But another dragon said that he had seen such a thing—smoke rising up through a hole in the snow.

<And how would we find this place?> the green-black dragon asked. <The sea is large. We could fly until we dropped and never catch sight of it.>

I swallowed. This I had prepared for, although it was the chanciest part of my plan. <Skava will lead you there,> I said. <Only . . . she does not yet know the way. I will direct her, but . . .> I hesitated. <I need to speak further with Kazan before I can do so—>

The convocation erupted in an explosion of smoke. I caught fragments of meaning—<A trick! A trap! She seeks only to escape!>—and I feared for a moment that they would flame at me. But then the green-black dragon began to speak. I heard it in my head: soothing sounds, directed not at me but at her kyn. Gradually the smoke dissipated and tempers ebbed. The green-black dragon turned to me and said, <How can we know you speak truly?>

<You can discover for yourselves. You needn't come within bowshot of me—Skava can fly to meet you and lead you there.>

The green-black dragon snorted. <This plan serves a bit too closely your wish to escape.>

<The bird is her slave!> This from another dragon.

<She's *not* my slave,> I said. <She's with you now.> I nodded toward the green dragon on whose back Skava perched. <When she comes to me, she does so of her own will.>

The voices arose again, so dense with words that I could not unravel them. At last the green-black dragon said, <We will ponder this now,> and I knew that I was dismissed.

I pulled my cloak around me and huddled on my island, listening as the drone of dragon-talk throbbed in my bones. Voicing my plan had made me see how full of snags it was. It was a desperate plan.

And yet . . . the dragons *had* listened. . . .

Things must be worse with them than I had thought.

The conclave went on all through the day. Dragon voices eddied through my mind, sometimes calm, sometimes rising in temper to a smoking, tail-thumping exchange. The young dragons forsook their play and came to listen, cocking their heads one way and another as different dragons spoke, turning often to stare at me.

I tried to attend to the thread of the debate, but the tide of opinion turned so often, and their words came so thick and intermingled that my mind veered often onto its own course, dreaming of a time when I could return to the king's steading—to the mews, to Corwyn and Rath and Myrra. And Kazan . . . I would see him again. . . .

At last I came up out of a doze to the whipcrack of my name in my mind. I looked up to see all the dragons staring at me.

<We will see what this land is, and whether it is to our liking,> the green-black dragon said. <You will return to your kyn and speak to this Kazan. Go with him to a place near the sea, where no men are about. Then call my name.>

She paused, and I sensed her reluctance to entrust me with her name.

<Byrn,> she said at last. <Call Byrn. But three of you only: Kazan, the bird, and you. *With no others.*>

I breathed in deep. So they agreed to it. This was the beginning.

<This night we move from this lair to another. But when you call, we will come.>

And then the dragons were moving toward the mouth of the cave. <Go,> Byrn commanded me.

I hesitated. <Where?>

<To your kyn. Go *now.*>

<But . . . food . . . I will need . . .>

Byrn flamed at my feet. I jumped back. Sparks sprayed out on the rock where I had stood before.

<Go.>

I snatched up pack and skis and clambered down from my perch into the press of dragons, terrified lest they would step on me or crush me among them. But their great talons moved neatly over and around me. Struggling into my pack, I felt a blast of hot breath just behind.

Byrn. Prodding me forward.

I heard wind gusts ahead as dragons launched themselves from the cave, but I could see nothing but a mass of dragon bodies before me, until one only remained. Then it was gone, too—first falling, then pumping and rising in the night.

And I stood at the edge of a precipice with Byrn breathing her hot breath down my neck. "I can go no farther!" I cried. I heard a snort of dragony laughter, felt the heat of it in the air above my head. Then I was gripped from behind. I heard the ripping of cloth, felt talons glide across my skin, and then my feet lifted off the ground and my stomach pitched into my throat.

We were flying.

The shock of cold was like a dive into icy water. Wind whipped my hair about my face and thundered in my ears; tears streamed out from the corners of my eyes. My stomach leapt into my throat. I felt the walls of the mountain lurch up past me, saw the snowfields come swimming up.

The whoosh of a wingbeat; the world tipped and gradually sank. We were rising. I let out my breath, only now aware that I had been holding it. As we banked round in a wide, slanting circle, I saw a fluid sweep of dragons flying north. In another moment we had turned away.

My shift and gown and the straps of my pack had all bunched up together in my armpits. A choking wad of fabric chafed at my throat. Byrn had seized my pack and cape and gown so that I hung down from her, unable to see anything above me save for the dark expanse of her underbelly and the black-veined undersides of her wings. But beneath my dangling feet the earth poured by: sharp crags and smooth valleys, cast into long shadows by a slip of a moon. Eddies of air threaded past—some warmer, others piercingly cold—like currents in the sea. I heard a faint tintinnabulation of bells. Skava. On an upbeat of Byrn's wings I caught a glimpse of her.

Slowly, my mind began to settle, began to work its way out of its shock. Byrn was taking me to the king's steading. That must be where we went.

Now I could make out the black of the sea curving away in the distance. Way off to the southwest I saw a glimmering of lights.

Yes. The steading.

It looked so small down there in the middle of the wide, curving earth. Like a hill of ants. Small wonder the dragons held us in contempt.

At once I was flooded with a strange, calm joy. In this hushed space, where I could hear only the wind and the beating of dragon wings and the faint, silvery jingling of Skava's bells . . . it was as if I could see the whole wide world laid out for me.

I could not hide forever from Orrik. I would speak to him, I would *persuade* him of what I must do—and lay claim to my place in the world.

And then the ground was rushing up—closer and closer—until it seemed certain we would collide with it. But we did not. At the last moment the talons slipped away from me and my feet were breaking through a crust of snow. And Byrn was a breath in the air, a shadow, gliding up into the night and away.

<You and your bird and Kazan. No others!>

Now Skava was swooping down to me. I held out my arm; she alit. I teased up her breast feathers, tethered her jesses to her leash, and then began to walk.

I gave wide berth to the courtyard buildings, keeping well outside the torchlight. It was no great feat to slip by the sentries. I heard them murmuring near the high hall, and crept near enough to count. Four men. The usual number. Suspecting nothing, they kept a lax watch.

I *would* put my case to Orrik—but not now. Best to find Corwyn first, discover how the land lay. Perhaps he would intercede for me with the king.

Between the storehouses I could see the flickerings of the soldiers' fires. I only hoped no dog would catch our scent and raise the alarm. I passed behind the stables and the byre but stopped in the lee of the cow shed. A trickle of yellow light ran across the hard-packed snow in the barnyard from the windows in the mews.

Corwyn. He must be awake.

I moved cautiously forward, restraining my eagerness.

A crunch in the snow behind me. I whirled around.

A sentry!

"Halt there! What—" In that instant I saw the changes wash across his face: recognition, and then shock.

Panicked, I bolted for the mews. But he came after, caught me from behind. "What are you—" I pulled away from him; he cursed, grabbed my free arm, twisted it behind me, and yanked it painfully up.

"I have her!" he called. "The dragon girl is here!"

Chapter 20

None more unkind than kin.

—KRAGISH PROVERB

V oices.

A burst of them from the warriors' tents and then many more from the courtyard behind me. For an instant I thought I saw Corwyn outlined in the doorway of the mews. I called for him—but then folk were converging upon me from all directions. Globs of yellow torchlight floated among the long, wavering shadows. Running footfalls. Questions, murmurs, shouts. And then the torches were thrust before my face, blindingly bright. Now one man stood before me in the throng, but I could make out only the shape of him. I squinted to see his face. "Corwyn?" I asked, and then his face came clear.

Not Corwyn.

Rog.

"*You!*" he said, with such force that I started; Skava hissed and struck at him with her foot.

Rog jumped back, held up his hand to shield his face. "Get it! Get the bird away!"

And someone was cutting through the leash—was it Corwyn? I could not see—and then Skava was gone.

Rog said something to the sentry who held me, and then *he* was holding me, twisting my arm behind my back. "Corwyn!" I called. I thought I heard his voice, but Rog jerked my arm up higher than before and shoved me through the crowd toward the courtyard. Pain shot upward to my shoulder; I stooped forward to ease it.

We picked up folk as we went until we were in the vanguard of a shadowy horde of soldiers, housecarls, children, bondmaids, and dogs, all marching through the trampled snow. Then a jinking of keys: Gudjen appeared at my side. "Where have you *been?*" she demanded. But her eyes showed real concern. She ordered Rog to release me and, when he did not, kept up a constant, carping rail at him.

As we approached the high hall, I saw limned in wavering torchlight the figure of the king. He stood with arms folded before him, waiting for the commotion to come and make itself known. But my glance slid away from Orrik's face—for beside him stood Kazan.

The trader walked rapidly forward some few steps, then checked his stride. And all the while his eyes did not leave my face.

"Kara!" Orrik said wonderingly. "We thought you dead. Kazan followed your traces to where the snow had buried you. . . ."

He trailed off, looked speculatively at Kazan.

So it *had* been he.

"I did run from you," I told Orrik. "And I repent me of any . . . hardship I caused. But I returned of my own will, and now, if you will hear me out, I have a plan——"

"Hog swill!" Rog roared. "I caught her skulking about the barnyard, Orrik. She had no intent to come to you. She kicked the guard—bloodied his shin!—to get away. I'll lock her up now until we resolve what to do with her."

"Let her speak!" Gudjen said. "I for one would like to discover how she escaped from a snow grave and where she has bided these past ten days."

"You've harkened to this country wench long enough. She's a witch, Orrik! Any fool could have seen it from the start!"

"Do you call me a fool, then, brother?" Orrik's voice was soft, dangerous.

Rog did not answer but glowered back.

"I must speak to you alone—with Corwyn and Kazan only," I besought the king. "There are things that I must tell you—things that others must not hear."

"There is nothing this girl says that *I* may not hear," Gudjen said, indignant.

"Give me your keys," Rog commanded his sister. "I'm locking her up."

Orrik faced him grimly. "Release her."

"I will not. She's a witch."

"Do you defy me?"

"You'll never slay those dragons, Orrik. You let these *women* lead you about like a harnessed mule. If I were king, I'd have five dragon heads mounted on the wall by now—and I'd be bedding Signy every night."

The king's nod was almost imperceptible. Four hearth companions came at Rog so swiftly that he had not time to make a move. They scuffled briefly, wrenching my arm worse than before, and then I was free and Rog held prisoner.

"You'll *never* slay them!" Rog said. "Signy will be a barren hag before ever you do." He stood with head lowered, eyes smoldering.

"Lock him in a storeroom," Orrik said. "I'll see to him later."

"You can't do this!" Rog stormed. "I'm the prince! I have a following of my own! You'll live to regret this, brother!"

The king motioned for me to follow, wheeled round, and strode within the hall.

Kazan came first into the hall after being summoned by Orrik. He bowed to the king and, saying no word, took my hand and looked square into my eyes. There was a bright, glad stillness within me, broken only by the beating of my heart.

Then Corwyn burst in, enveloped me in a huge bear hug. Neither did he speak—nor I. Words would not do.

Orrik sat in his high seat, lumined by the flame of a single torch, when I began my tale. There were but the four of us, as I had requested—Orrik, Corwyn, Kazan, and I—but a guard stood away by the door.

"He will hear us," I said to Orrik, looking at the guard.

"No matter. He is *my* man and knows how to keep his mouth shut."

The king heeded well when I told what had passed with me but grew restless when I put forward my plan. His foot began to tap; he rose, paced to and fro, rubbing his beard. When I came to the part of directing Skava, he rounded on Corwyn.

"Do you credit this . . . *directing?*" he asked.

"I have seen her do it," Corwyn said. "I would not have believed it had I not witnessed it with my own two eyes, but I can vouch for it beyond question."

"But to a far place, a place she's never seen?" Orrik persisted.

Corwyn hesitated. "That I do not know."

"I directed Skava well beyond my sight when I was in the cave," I said.

"And you know for certain she arrived at the place where you sent her?" Orrik looked skeptical.

"I . . . believe so."

"But you don't know."

"No, but—"

Orrik resumed his pacing. Behind his back Kazan shot me a look I could not decipher. And now, even as I tried desperately to persuade him, Orrik was shaking his head. "No," he said, still pacing. "No, it will not do. It is too chancy. Too happenstance."

"But two-score dragons!" I said. "Think of the toll in human blood. How much better to meet your ends and theirs at once! Put an end to the blood feud—and to their raids on sheep."

Kazan spoke up. "In my land we have a saying, your grace: 'Mutton speaks louder than glory.' In my view, folk in *any* land care more for the food on their boards than for the glory of their kings. If you can halt the depredations of dragons by any means, they will thank you for it."

Orrik stood before me. "I have said no," he said. "And now you know how to call them . . . we *will* end their depredations. We will finish them. Finish them all. Let Rog prate of harnessed mules *then*!"

"No," I said, horror mounting inside me. "No, I won't. I *can't*. They have spared my life—twice. And this plan—*it* would bring you glory—"

"I have told you—no! You will call them for me to slay."

"I will not."

"*You* defy me, too? Outright?"

"Yes."

"Devil's spawn! What *is* it about this day? First my brother and then you . . . Well, I cannot brook it! You *will* call them—I will compel you to it by one means or another."

You will *not*, I thought. You can kill me, but you can't force me to call them. I stood mute, held by Orrik's gaze. Out of the corner of my eyes I caught a flash of something metal at Kazan's side.

At once there came a pounding barrage at the door. "Your grace!" came a voice from without. "Rog has escaped with a band of warriors and is bound for Romjek. He will put aside his wife, he says, and seek the hand of Signy!"

Chapter 21

A red sprat, dragged across the holt cat's trail,
will send the hounds astray.

—KRAGISH HUNTERS' LORE

"To Signy? Rog's gone to Signy?" Orrik's voice rose in alarm. "Enter!"

The door opened and a throng of warriors hastened within. One strode forward, clutching in his hand a leaf of parchment. "He left this."

Orrik snatched it, moved near the torch, and began to read. " 'Since you will not avenge Signy's brother's death,' " he mumbled, " 'I will make suit to her myself.' "

Orrik looked up, dumbfounded. I feared he would march me to the seacoast this very moment and demand that I call the dragons. "She'll never have him," he said grimly when he found his voice at last. "But I can't have him charging up there, making me look the fool. Summon my hearth companions to the courtyard," he commanded. "I go now to muster the troops."

He took two steps toward the door, then stopped and turned to me. "Oh, and . . . best keep her under guard until I return." Two men seized my arms.

"You can't do this!" Kazan shouted. "She has done nothing against you; she has returned of her own will."

"I do what I will in my own kingdom," Orrik retorted. "And besides, with Rog loose, she is not safe." He paused, seemed to soften, and turned to me. "I . . . regret this, Kara. But you have deserted me and defied me; I can trust you no longer." To the guards he said, "She may have whatsoever she desires, save for her freedom. Treat well with her or you will answer to me."

Then he hurried from the hall, pursued by Kazan, who, protesting loudly, clung to him as a tick clings to a dog. I heard Kazan call him "tyrant," and the king's angry reply— "Take care you do not wear out your welcome and find *yourself* under guard,"—before their voices dissolved amid the courtyard din.

And now my guards propelled me into that din. Folk were rushing all about in the light of moving torches: bearing food from the kitchenhouse and ale from the brewery; strapping on swords and packs and skis; shouting, babbling, wailing. They did not smile at me as I passed. I had thrown away their good favor when I ran from Orrik's camp. Perhaps it could be regained if I would consent to hunt dragons again. But that I could not do.

I looked about for Gudjen, but she, too, had deserted me. Only Corwyn stayed close, assuring me as we made our way through the throng that he would get me out some way. Asking me if there were aught I wished.

"I wish," I said wearily, "that I had never laid eyes on this treacherous place."

The whale-oil lamp within the storehouse stank evilly, giving off more smoke than light. A small brazier stood at the center of the room; the guards had lighted it before they left, but it shed little warmth. Although I was not permitted visitors, I heard the voices of Corwyn and Kazan from time to time and caught glimpses of their faces as the guards thrust provisions through the doorway: blankets and bolsters, a brew-bladder, packets of food. Inside one of these packets I found a moist, sticky clump of Kazan's dried yellow fruits.

I was too restless to eat, or even to sit. I paced the rushes, listening to the sounds in the courtyard, trying to fathom what passed there. Shoutings. Clankings. The whoosh and scrape of men on ski. But in time these sounds subsided, and I surmised that the king's contingent had departed.

The brazier, at long last, began to put out a trickle of heat. I settled myself down beside it but leapt again to my feet at a new sound. Corwyn's voice. Raised in . . . alarm? In pain?

"What is it?" I called to the guard. "What's befallen?"

I heard murmurings, then, "Nothing to trouble you," someone said.

"But what *is* it?" I persisted. "Is Corwyn hurt?"

They would not respond.

And so I resumed my pacing, plagued now by more questions than before. Why had Corwyn called out? Would the king overtake Rog ere he reached Signy? Would they do battle? And who would prevail when all was done: Orrik? Or—the gods help me—Rog?

If Rog gained command, I was doomed. There was no

judiciousness to Rog; he saw all as a contest of force. And he despised me for the trouble I had caused.

But Orrik . . . Perhaps he might yet be persuaded. . . .

Footfalls. Many footfalls. And among them a clanking of keys.

Gudjen.

I heard voices outside the door; it was flung wide for Gudjen to enter; she shut it close behind her.

"What was that I heard?" I asked. "What did they do to Corwyn?"

"Corwyn is . . . unharmed," Gudjen said. Her voice sounded tired. In the dim lamplight, her face looked lined and bleak.

"Then what did I hear?"

Gudjen ignored my question and seemed, for a moment, to gaze at a point well beyond the guardhouse wall. "I had such hopes for you, Kara," she said. "That you would make it possible for Orrik to be a hero and win Signy's hand. That the two lands—Krag and Romjek—would unite. That there would soon be an heir. . . .

"*I* wanted the rearing of that heir, the next king. For Orrik is not strong—not as our father was strong. Not as he needs to be strong. And Rog is rash and vindictive—an idiot! The fates forbid that ever he should be king. But with the rearing of Orrik's heir . . . I could have *made* that child into the king we need. We would prosper and win other lands in battle until we commanded an empire such as the world has never seen. And hunger among the Krags would be the stuff of ancient tales.

"But you—" She turned to me reproachfully. "It seems you love dragons more than your own king and country. Or is it only that you fear them?" She studied me a moment before going on. "Well, at any pass, Rog has made his move, and for once it is canny. He knows *my* weaknesses, and yours as well, I deem. . . ."

"But there is a way, that I told to Orrik," I said. "You could yet have your heir to rear—"

"Rog has taken Myrra and the boy Rath," Gudjen said harshly. "He has sworn to slay them unless you go to him and call the dragons. He *would* kill them—I think—his pride is so far crushed. And I cannot find the strength in me to let him."

The guards were reluctant to release me, but Gudjen bullied and threatened, declaring, "*I* wear the keys to this steading," and at last swept me out of their ward. She bustled me through the courtyard to the high hall, explaining all that had passed. Rog had not, I learned, gone to Signy after all. That had been a ruse to send Orrik and his men on the wrong course. Rog had departed with his troops to a secret place where now they awaited me. It was I he had wanted—to call down the dragons. To make a hero out of him.

"Rog has sent some few of his men to fetch you," Gudjen said, "and if we refuse outright to release you, he may yet carry out his threat to kill the children. So put him off—by whatever means you can. I'll send for Orrik; he'll come for you."

"But how? We'll be well away before ever he returns. He'll never find us!"

"I'll have you followed. Leave all to me."

Now we approached the high hall where a cluster of men stood arguing, Kazan and Corwyn among them. Gudjen accosted the chief sentry—there were five or six sentries, I saw—and straightaway fell into another stormy exchange. "The king gave clear orders to keep her," the sentry said, "and I will not release her to Rog, who has become the king's enemy."

"The circumstance has changed," Gudjen retorted, "and I know best what Orrik would do were he here. Would *you* read his mind? Would you pay the price of reading it wrongly?"

"I do only what he commanded," the sentry said stubbornly. "He will not hold that against me."

"And I say he will—and I know him the better. And in either case you will have *my* wrath to contend with for a surety." Gudjen fixed him with a baleful eye. He held her gaze until it seemed that he could bear it no longer, for he sullenly stood aside.

Kazan and Corwyn were still arguing with the men who had come for me. Both the trader and the falconer pleaded to be taken hostage as well. But, "I know of your plans for the dragons," one man said to Kazan, and at once I knew him as the guard who had held the high hall door while I told Orrik of my plan.

"If you have blood and not ice in your veins, take me in exchange for my daughter," Corwyn pleaded. "She is innocent of all, she . . ." He choked, seemingly unable to go on. It tore at me to see him so. Kazan laid a hand on Corwyn's shoulder, said something low in his ear.

Then one of the men was spinning me around, binding my hands behind my back. He shoved me along the trodden-snow path to the fjord. I turned to look for Kazan and Corwyn, but they were nowhere to be seen. Nor Gudjen, either.

They had left me.

Chapter 22

As well try to herd dragons.

—COMMON KRAGISH

REMARK ON A

FUTILE ACT

We made our way down to the wharf. I trod gingerly on the slippery path, my balance hampered because my hands, lashed behind my back, could not aid me. From time to time my captor dealt me a shove to speed me; I had to scramble to recover my footing.

The downward slope before us, deep in snow, dissolved into shadow all around. A ghostly pall of smoke-frost clung to the surface of the fjord.

We had come nearly to the wharf when I heard a thud and then splintering sounds. I strained my eyes to see.

I could barely make out the ships, gray shadows on the lighter gray of smoke-frost. But there was something . . . odd about them. They rode low in the water—too low. All of them—longships, knarrs, fishing boats.

Something moved inside one of the boats. A man. He held something, something that gleamed faintly. An axe? I drew in breath. Was he chopping holes . . . in the bottoms of the ships? But the guard . . .

"Did you take care of the trader's ship as well?" The sentry's voice came from behind me.

"No need," the man said. "They're replanking the hull. It would sink like a stone if they tried to sail it now."

He *was* sinking the boats! They must have killed the ships' guard—or he had joined them. I let out my breath, felt all within me sag. No one could follow on foot. The terrain was too rough.

"Let's go, then." I was shoved in the direction of a small sailless bark I had not marked before.

This bark alone rode high in the water. The man pushed me again. I turned around and looked daggers at him, but he only laughed. "Glare at me all you want, *dragon girl*. With your hands bound and no falcon to hide behind, your wings are well and truly clipped."

All the men rowed; I wedged myself uncomfortably in the prow. My wrists and arms began to ache. None would tell me whither we were bound; they hardly spoke at all. Only the plash of oars and the creaking of wood and the deep, far-off rumble of the sea broke silence. Behind us, through the mist, I could see a faint glimmering of torches. The steading. Each stroke of the oars dragged me farther from it, farther from warmth and friends and help.

The sea's roar, growing louder as we neared, put fear in me that we would attempt to sail it in this frail bark. But we did not. We lay in at last on a rocky beach at the north shore of the fjord, just before it met with the sea. The men portaged the bark around a snowy headland and up the coast to the shores of a small bay.

And there before us burned the fires of an armed camp. Rog's camp.

Someone called out, "I have her!" The camp erupted in a flurry of movement. The fires were doused. Men—a score of them—swarmed toward us out of the mist, and I marked for the first time the longship drawn up upon the beach. They must have stolen it earlier under cover of night and fog.

"Get in," my sentry said, pushing me toward the ship.

I waded through the shallows; someone lifted me over the gunwale as I could not climb in myself without use of my hands. Then a shriek: "Kara!"

I turned and was accosted by Myrra with a force that nearly knocked me off my feet. Her hands, I saw, were bound before her. She leaned against me, sobbing, burying her face in my cloak. I ached to hold her, to stroke her hair, to wipe away her tears. I looked beyond, to Rath. His hands, too, were bound before him. He smiled up at me with wide, hopeful eyes as if I were a savior who had come to deliver him from all harm.

"I can't . . ." I said softly to him, over Myrra, and then swallowed. "I can't make them come down low enough to please Rog. You must know this. I can't . . . *make* them come at all." Rath stood silent for a long moment. The hope in his eyes dimmed. He nodded gravely, and *that* tore at me nearly as much as Myrra's sobs, for it seemed he had aged ten years.

Rog spoke no word to me but went straight to man the steering oar and began shouting orders. The mast was raised. Myrra, Rath, and I huddled together for comfort and warmth between the rows of crewmen.

The smoke-frost gradually dissipated; the sky grew lighter in the south, abating from black to purple to deep, rich shades of blue. Still, the wind blew bitter cold and the sea spray bit like ice. Through our plumes of frosted breath the land loomed white, save for a smooth, dark fringe of sand.

It was daylight by the time we put ashore—on a rock-strewn bay bounded by cliffs and faced by an offshore island.

One of the soldiers was herding Myrra and Rath and me across the sand toward the cliffs when Rog approached and halted us. "Call the dragons!" he commanded me.

"My lord, you must understand," I said carefully, "that I can call them—I *will* so if you wish it. But I cannot compel them to come down low enough to be slain."

"You can! I have seen it. Do you think me blind? Do you think me witless?" He drew so near that I could smell the rankness of his breath, could see the bloodshot lines in his pale eyes. There was an overwrought look to them, a too-bright intensity.

"No, my lord," I hastened to assure him. "Only . . . they have learned from that time before not to come near."

"*Learned?* They don't learn. They do as their lust wills— or as black arts command. You have the bidding of them. Tell them," he said, and now a crafty look stole across his face, "tell them you're sending them to this . . . *land of fire beneath the earth*." He paused, measuring me. The guard, I thought. The one by the door when I told Orrik my plan. He was Rog's man now.

"Oh, yes," Rog went on, chuckling, "I do know of this. I know all your plans. They will come to you. Now, *call!*"

"If you know my plans, you know also they will come to me when Kazan and Skava are with me—but no others. They will not come when an army is near."

"So we hide beneath the cliffs. *Call!*"

"It is daylight! They come out only at deepest night!"

"*Call*, plague you! Or your friends—" Rog spun round, surprisingly quickly, and, before I could move to stop him, clouted Rath hard in the stomach. With a gasp of escaping breath, Rath doubled over and fell backward onto the sand. He lay curled—eyes squeezed shut, hands clutched against his stomach—but he uttered never a cry.

"Don't!" I screamed, lunging at Rog. Someone grabbed my bound hands and held me. I stood glowering at Rog, choking back the bitter bile that rose in my throat.

"It will go worse with him if you refuse," Rog said. "And with the girl as well. I will hold them under water until all the bubbles stop."

"You would not," I said softly. "You are yet human."

"And you would wager their lives on that?"

I minded me of what Gudjen had said: *He would kill them—his pride is so far crushed.* "I will call," I replied at last, "but this I swear: If ever you lay hands on them, I will tell the dragons to go back and never come to me more. No—I will tell them to burn you until your skin turns black and your fat crackles. And I don't give gull's droppings what befalls me after that."

Rog laughed. I wrenched myself out of the warrior's grasp and came away so easily that I knew Rog must have signaled him to let me go. I stumbled across the hard, wet sand toward the water, then turned back again. "And don't look for them before deepest night," I shouted, "for they will not come before, and nothing I can do will compel them!"

* * *

Now there was a clamoring in my mind and I did not know what to do. I stood facing out to sea, gulping in the chill salt air, trying to collect my thoughts. I could feign calling the dragons and no one would know—not until deepest night. Perhaps I might keep Rog hanging beyond even that, but not by much, I guessed. And then . . . Would he carry out his threat?

No. He could not be that far lost.

Or could he?

If I could at least give him sight of a dragon. That would show that I had *tried* to do his will, even if I could not do all. At the very least, it would buy me time.

But time for what?

Orrik had no ships and no way to know where we were.

The dragons wouldn't come down too near—that I knew. They didn't trust me that far. As well they shouldn't. For it would be a betrayal, calling them now. And I . . . balked at betraying them. Did not *want* to betray them. I wanted to rise above their contempt.

I heard footfalls in the sand behind me. Myrra. She looked beseechingly at me, tears streaking down her face. I knelt down to her; she leaned her head against my shoulder and gave a little sob. Her hood fell back; her hair was damp and smelled of salt. Likely Rog had bade her come to me, a cynical ploy, and yet . . . it had its effect.

Better small hope than none.

I looked away, to north and east, above the cliffs.

<Byrn!> I called. <Come. Byrn.>

There was a tingling in my mind, like to that I had felt when I called Flagra.

It was done.

* * *

The birds came then, birds nowhere in the sky before—
ravens, ptarmigan, redpoll, gulls. We settled into the lee
of the cliffs beside a pitiful fire of damp twigs and branches,
which gave little warmth.

Waiting.

Rog's mood changed as we waited, swinging wildly from
elation to sullenness to anger. He spoke of the many slights
dealt him by his father and mother, his brother and sister.
Never again, he said. Now they would know his worth. He
spilled his plot in bits; he would not respond to questions but
sometimes harangued at his men and sometimes muttered to
himself and sometimes railed at me until gradually I pieced
together what he intended.

Rog spoke not of loving Signy but only of the power she
could bring him. He thought to avenge her brother's death
and more: to kill all the dragons that had long raided his
countrymen's sheep and cows. Orrik's own warriors would
desert him and flock to Rog as the true hero, the powerful
one.

Rog had not, so far as I could tell, devised a way to rid
himself of his brother. But I had no doubt that Orrik would
not grace this world for long, if Rog had his way.

The longer he raved, the more frightened I became. He
had wagered all on this misbegotten venture. If he lost, would
he scruple to take down with him two children and a dragon
girl?

The sun set, but twilight lingered in the sky. The birds
flew desultorily above. And still Rog raved. My hands grew
numb with cold, the more so since they were bound behind
my back. I turned around and wiggled my fingers before the

fire to ward off frostbite. I had begged some furs for Myrra
and Rath; now they sat and watched me with great eyes. From
time to time I walked out from beneath the cliffs to search the
sky.

I could not see them.

I could not feel them.

One by one, the stars appeared.

A gust of wind. It whuffed against my ears and faintly
brushed my face. The birds began to swoop and cry. I looked
up and saw, beyond the offshore island, an eddy of birds.

No. Not birds. Though they seemed small as birds, there
was something odd about them . . . their shape . . . the way
they flew. There was a rumbling deep inside my bones.

A shiver crawled up my neck and prickled at my scalp.

<One man. No others. That was the promise you
made.>

Byrn's voice drove like a shaft through my skull. I cried
out; my head flinched downward and my shoulders hunched
convulsively to protect it.

"What is it?" Rog yelled, bursting out from beneath the
cliffs. "Are they come?"

"Go back!" I said. "They won't come if they see you."

"One other, you told Orrik. Don't try to trick me, Kara;
I know what you're about. Say I am Kazan." He came nearer,
stared into the sky. "Birds. Those are but birds." He turned
to me. "Birds came with them the last time, too. They—"

I shook my head. "Not birds. Dragons. I said I'd call
them, and I did."

"Dragons? Don't cozen me! They're much too small for
dragons!"

"They're far away! You see the shape of them, how they
fly?"

Rog squinted uncertainly into the twilight sky, turned back to me, then seemed to make up his mind. He ran back to the cliffs, shouting, "Dragons! They're here! Nock your arrows!"

<Is *he* the one you spoke of?> Byrn asked contemptuously.

I hesitated. I could not lie.

<No,> I said. <He is not. He took two young ones of my—my kyn . . . and threatens their lives. He would have killed them if I refused to call you. And I knew you would not trust me so far as to come down within bowshot, and so your kyn would be in no danger.>

I felt a wordless response that felt like nothing so much as a snort of pure contempt. <Humans!> The cluster of dragons shrank back.

<Wait!> I called. <Only show yourselves to him. Not within bowshot, but near enough that he can see . . .>

<You have betrayed us—*used* us. Why should we help you? You are *his* creature now. He tethers you, even as you tethered the falcon.>

<No I'm not, I—>

"Call them in close. Now!" Rog yelled.

"I'm trying! Only wait!"

I closed my eyes and sought Byrn with my mind, to beg her to come within clear sight. But I felt only an odd, unyielding force, something hard and shut against me. When I opened my eyes, the dragons had melted back into the thickening twilight; their rumblings had dwindled to a muted thrum.

I heard voices behind me; I turned around. The archers had lowered their bows. "Birds," one man said. "They were only birds."

And a murmur of "Birds" rippled through the company

190

of warriors. Someone snickered—and then all went suddenly silent. I turned to look at Rog, afraid.

"You'll pay for this," he said softly, and then louder, "Fetch me the boy! No, wait!" Rog held up his hand. "The girl," he said, turning to study my face. "*She* will be first."

"No," I said. "Don't. They were . . . They *are* dragons. You saw them, saw the shape of them, saw them *hovering* there so long. Birds do not—"

"Don't think you can fool me again! They were birds!"

Now one of the warriors came carrying Myrra under his arm. She kicked and screamed, but to no avail. "You won't do this," I said, more to comfort myself than to persuade him of it. "I know you. You are a warrior—yes—but not a murderer."

Rog gave me a hard, dead look. The man handed Myrra to him as easily as if she were a sack of grain. Rog waded into the surf.

"No!" I screamed, lunging forward. Pain arced up my arm. The warrior had seized it; he was holding me back.

And Rog was thigh-deep in the surf, was dropping Myrra, was grabbing her hair. I caught one quick glimpse of her face—white and drawn and pleading. "Wait!" I said. "I'll do anything, I'll call them, I'll make them come, I—"

"You should have done that before, instead of trying to dupe me. Now it's too late for *her*," Rog said, "so do it for the boy."

He shoved her head under the waves.

My scream tore at my throat.

He could not do this; he must be bluffing; he *would* let her up. . . .

But how if he did not?

<Byrn!> I called. I could barely see them now; they

191

were but specks in the darkening sky. <Come, please come. Just near enough that he can see you! Not for me—for her—for Myrra. She has done nothing—nothing! She is innocent of all!>

They were there—I knew it. I could hear the faint thrumming beneath the shrill cries of birds, beneath the hissing roar of the waves.

He still held her down. Could she hold out so long without breath?

Then . . . a tingling. <We will not be your targets—but I will tell you this. I see many men on ski, drawing near above the cliffs. And the bird, Skava, is nearer still.>

Chapter 23

Where have they gone
the old night-flyers,
fire-foes,
haunters of the heights?
Where have they gone
the ancient kyn of dragons?

—KRAGISH SKALD

Many men above the cliffs? And Skava . . . near?
I wrenched round to look back.

Nothing. Nothing but cliffs and snow and stars. If there were men, they were too far from us to help. But Skava . . . I could call . . .

<Skava, come! Come!> I scanned the gloom behind me. Nothing. There was nothing. But wait. . . .

A ghostly form, gliding down from the cliffs.

Skava.

Now to turn her, to bend her flight. I fixed my eyes upon Rog, studied his face. He was shouting; he still held Myrra down.

<Go,> I willed Skava. <Go.>

The thin current of her awareness trickled through my mind; I *directed* her toward Rog. I longed to turn to see her but dared not avert my gaze. Then there she was, skimming low across the edge of my vision, across the sand—straight for Rog's face. Even in the dim light I saw it change, saw the fear seize hold. He swore, threw up his hands, staggered away, and then he and the bird were one: man-screams and bird-screams; wings and hands and claws all flailing together. Blood. There was blood. And something in the water . . . dark, with a round, pale face.

Myrra.

She lived.

She tottered through the surf, stumbled, fell, disappeared under water, and then she was up again.

"Myrra!"

I tried to twist away from my captor, but he held me fast. I looked up at the circling birds and called, <Come!> They wheeled, swooped down toward me, a rabble of squawking birds. I heard the man's yelp, felt his grip detach from my arm. I released the birds with my mind and ran for Myrra.

Shouts. Rapid footfalls across the sand: Rog's men. "Get it! Get the bird!" Rog was screaming.

<Come, Skava!> I called, and just as I reached Myrra, I heard the breath of the falcon's wingbeat, felt the impact of her weight on my shoulder.

Myrra was staggering, choking up water. She fell to her knees in the receding foam. "Get up, lamblet," I said. "Come on." Another wave—so cold, it burned. If only my hands weren't tied. I would scoop her up; I would run.

They would be here now, any moment—Rog's men.

A shout. A whistling noise. I ducked, but then, "The king!" someone yelled.

I spun round to look.

Arrows. Arrows raining down from the cliffs. The tiny dark forms of men stood silhouetted against the purple sky.

I did not stop to marvel how Orrik had found us but went on coaxing Myrra out of the water. She could scarcely walk. She gripped my arm in her two bound hands; it was slow—impossibly slow. One good thing: No one pursued us now. For the moment, at least, all was confusion. Rog's men were running, shouting, loosing arrows at Orrik's men, who in turn swarmed down through crannies in the cliffs, keeping up a steady stream of arrows.

A small fleeing figure caught my eye, cutting in and out among the men, among the arrows.

Rath!

He reached us as we came out of the wet, sucking sand onto harder ground, and in his bound hands he held a miracle: a dagger. I would have hugged him if I could. It was bliss when the rope around my wrists fell away and I could move my sore arms before me; but I had not leisure to revel in it, for arrows were falling dangerously near. I sawed through Rath's bonds and had nearly severed the last stubborn threads of Myrra's when I heard Rath scream and then Skava pushed off; she was flying. Rath clutched at his shoulder; something jutted out between his fingers.

An arrow.

He was hit.

I froze.

"Hurry!" Rath said through gritted teeth and began to run southward down the shore. My hand commenced sawing, but my mind stayed stuck. The last thread came loose; I picked up Myrra and ran stumblingly across the sand. My breath came ragged as I followed Rath, wondering that he could move so fast with an arrow in him. Then a shout, two shouts. Two men were pelting down the beach toward us from the south.

I knew Corwyn first, knew the stout shape of him, knew by the way he held the falcon—it was Skava—on his fist.

And before him . . . Kazan!

A sob of relief shuddered through me. I ran, eyes fixed on the two men until Kazan was lifting Myrra from me, giving her to Corwyn; until Kazan took me in his arms. His voice was a breath in my ear: "Kara." And I would have stayed there longer, but for Rath. . . .

"Rath is hurt," I said, "an arrow . . . his shoulder . . ."

And we came apart. Kazan bent to look at the arrow, then picked up Rath. Corwyn thrust out his fist for me to take Skava—I did so, praising her softly—and then we all ran south along the beach to where a small bark lay fetched up on the sand.

Corwyn laid Myrra gently within, and Kazan set Rath beside her. The two men dragged the boat into the shallows. Kazan bade me get in while he and Corwyn pushed it out into deeper water. Then they climbed in, too; Kazan rowed through the worst of the surf. The bark reared like an unbroken steed; waves crashed against us, breaking into spray. I tucked Skava inside my cloak and bailed.

When we reached the calmer waters beyond the surf, the men raised the mast and hoisted the sail. Then Kazan manned the steering oar, and Corwyn tended to Rath. There was a heap of furs in the prow where I sat with Myrra; I plucked out three dry ones and set about stripping off her sodden clothes and swaddling her in fur. She smiled, leaned back against me, gripped one of my fingers hard.

"This bark," I shouted to Kazan over the whipping wind. "I thought they destroyed all the boats."

"It is my ship's bark," he replied, grinning. "It was stowed in a corner of the shiphouse, and they never thought to look."

"So where are we going?"

"I know a place where you can hide. Orrik is still wroth with you for thwarting him; and if Rog prevails, you will not be safe anywhere in the Kragish lands. I will take you away—"

"No," I said. The word came without my thinking, without my willing it.

Kazan flinched, said nothing for a moment. Then, "You may not wish to go with me, Lady, but for now I am your only hope."

"It isn't that I don't want to go with you," I said. "Only . . . I have promised . . . to the dragons—"

"To send them to the northern land? Well and good! But choose another time, Lady—when we are not caught fast between two armies!"

"But we're not between them now. Take me . . ." I looked out across the heaving waters to where the island loomed gray against the sky. "Take me to that island. I'll call from there."

"And when one side or the other prevails, how safe do you think we will be? There's a longship under those cliffs, and it can outstrip this puny bark in the beat of a falcon's wing. We need to be well away—and soon!"

There was reason in what he said. And yet . . . I felt a

trembling deep in the marrow of my bones, too low for hearing. I stroked Myrra's hair as I scanned the sky, trying to see through the darkness.

Nothing. I saw nothing. And yet I knew that they were there.

"They won't come another time," I said to Kazan. "I betrayed them, can't you see? I made *use* of them. But they're out there now. I have to do this *now*."

"Out *where*? I don't see them."

"If you're *afraid,* only tell me what this land is like and I'll call them by myself."

Kazan, struggling with the sail, glared at me. "Well, call them from here," he said.

"I promised there would be no others by but you and Skava. I broke that promise before and will not again. I need to call now."

"Kazan," Corwyn said, looking up from where he tended Rath, "the shaft has snapped; I need to cut the arrow out and I can't do it in this pitching craft. Myrra . . . she needs a fire to warm her. We *must* get to land soon, and the island is safest."

Kazan swore softly, reset the oar, and turned the bark.

It was a rough passage to the island. The wind beat at our ears and flung stinging salt spray in our faces; the bark tossed on the waves like a hoarnut shell.

Kazan told me in snatches what had passed at the steading: how Corwyn had overheard one of Rog's men speak of "north, up the coast"; how Gudjen had sent a messenger to intercept the king; how Corwyn and he had found the bark and followed through the smoke-frost. "We lost you in the open sea but found you again by the birds," Kazan said, "as the king must have done as well."

When at last we reached the island, Kazan did not put in at the leeward shore but instead rounded the southernmost end and lay in at a small cliff-bound cove. We dragged the bark up onto the sand and carried Rath and Myrra to a sheltered nook in the rock. We nested them in furs and started a fire. Then Kazan and I—with Skava tethered on my fist—searched along the beach until we found a steep animal track that offered a way up.

The wind tore at us as we climbed. In the deepening twilight, it was hard to pick out footholds. Scree rattled out from beneath our feet; we slipped on glazed-over patches of ice. Kazan offered to hold Skava for me, but I could not give her up—not yet.

We came out on a high, flat bluff. I was resettling Skava on my fist when Kazan suddenly seized my arm. He pointed behind me, toward the mainland.

A white gash of foam in the sea. And above it—a dark sail.

The king?

Or his brother?

In either case, we had not much time.

I drew in breath and called.

They must have been near, for the wind picked up sharply. It roared in my ears, whipped my hair about my face, stirred up a fine, whirling flurry of snow. A tumult of birds converged in the darkness overhead. And then I saw them in the distance: first specks and then blotches and then dragons—clearly dragons—surging above the sea like breakers rolling for shore.

They circled round the island, glittering, winged eels

that filled the sky. Deep in my bones, their thrumming rumbled. Blue breath-flames burst and faded, leaving pale, smoky ghosts like spider-spin in the air. They had all come—the kyn entire. I knew this without troubling to count.

I could feel the cool, thin thread of Skava's excitement. She gazed intently at the dragons, leaning forward. I scratched her feet and reproached her: "So eager to leave me now, are you?" She burbled in her throat, nibbled at my fingers. There was a bright, sharp pang in my chest.

I nodded to Kazan.

He began to speak of this northern land, and it took form in my mind, as though emerging from a fog or a dream: a throng of mountain hulks, girt round by valleys near the sea. Wisps of steam arose from this land, as if the earth itself were breathing. Kazan told me of one mountain he had seen: squat and blocky, topped by a cloudy plume. Something familiar . . . Had I seen it before?

Yes. In the steamhouse. With Gudjen. It came clear for me now.

And Skava was bating . . .

"Hush," I said, settling her back on my fist. Kazan handed me his dagger; carefully I slit through her bewits to remove her silver bells. She would not need them now. Then I mocked myself inwardly, reflecting: She never did need them. *I* needed for her to have them.

The first jess fell away. I looked up at the dragons, still circling overhead. There was Byrn, and the green one Skava had befriended—the one with the notched back ridge. And there was my friend, the young one with the arrow scar.

Skava had a wild, longing look about her. I slipped the knife between her leg and the jess, cut through the leather, and, still holding the vision of that mountain peak in my mind, willed, <Go.>

She pushed off my wrist, streaked out across the sea. The kyn of dragons wheeled and gathered in a single, liquid movement. Then one was peeling away from the rest—the young red one, my friend. It came swooping down, straight for my head. Kazan yelled, yanked on my hand, dived to the ground; every instinct urged me to do the same. But I forced myself to stand erect as the dragon skimmed not a fingerlength above me, breathed a smoky sigh that stirred my hair.

Farewell.

He soared round to rejoin his kyn. Slowly they unfurled, stretched out in a dark, gleaming ribbon behind Skava.

Skava.

I watched her until she vanished in the deep purple sky: a tiny white speck, pursued by dragons. A great aching engulfed my heart. My companion she had been—my stout companion.

Then Kazan was tugging my hand. "Kara, let's go, *now*! They come!"

As I looked, a warrior appeared out of the darkness near the far edge of the bluff. He shouted; others sprang up beside him. They swarmed across the bluff; I ran.

Then a voice: "Kara, wait!"

It was Orrik.

I slipped my hand from Kazan's, turned around to face him.

"Kara, are you crazy? Run!" Kazan said, grabbing again for my hand.

"No."

"Kara, don't be rash. Orrik will be raging; no telling

what he will do. If we go now we can reach the bark and be well under way before he can get back to his longship."

"I can't . . . run anymore," I said. "You can go if you wish."

Kazan looked skyward as if to beseech the heavens against my folly. "Kara, be sensible—just this one time," he pleaded. "Don't throw away your life!"

"I *am* being sensible," I said. "I must stay and make my peace."

Chapter 24

Take these gifts and use them well.

—LINES FROM

RITUAL

MARRIAGE GIFT-GIVING,

KRAGLAND

Orrik barked out a command to his men; they halted. I could see him now, a lank, shadowed figure walking alone across the headland.

"Would you wait for me?" I asked Kazan and added, as he moved to come with me, "Here?" He checked his step, blew out a hard, frosty breath, nodded grimly.

I strained to see the king's countenance in the dusk as we drew near—trying to take measure of his mood. He stopped, folded his arms across his chest. "You defied me, Kara," he said. "I charged you not to send them away."

"I know."

He did seem angry, but there was no fire to it. Tired. More than all else, he seemed tired.

"I couldn't do them harm, your grace. And I feared you would force me to it. You . . . or Rog."

"Rog." Orrik looked out beyond me, the way the dragons had gone. All color had drained out of the sky; the stars gleamed distant and cold. Abruptly, Orrik turned back. "You needn't fret about Rog," he said harshly. "He's dead."

"D—dead?" I shouldn't have been so shocked, but it jolted me; the word stumbled on my tongue.

"Not by my own hand, though if another had not done it, it would like to have come to that. I did love him," Orrik said, looking at me accusingly, as if I would deny it. "But he craved to be king, and that office is open to one only. Always pushing, always challenging, always striving to prove himself my equal. Ever taking offense where none was intended." Orrik sighed.

"Well," he said and was silent a moment. "So you have me haltered and tied. I've sworn to avenge Signy's brother, but you have sent the dragons away—before all my men—making a fool of me."

"Did you tell others that you had forbidden me to send them away?"

"I had other matters on my mind! My own brother betrayed me and—"

"Hear what I mean, your grace. If you were to claim that I did *your* bidding in sending them away . . . many, I think, would count you as wise. Now all raids on livestock will cease. The ancient kyn of dragons . . . is gone."

Orrik rubbed his beard thoughtfully. "Was that *all* of them?"

"I . . . believe so. To dragons, *kyn* is both kind and kin. So dragon kyn to them means all beings of the dragon kind. And all are akin. To them we are human kyn—the human kind of beings—and they seem perplexed that we don't all treat with one another as kin."

"We don't treat with our *kin* as kin," Orrik muttered. He shook his head doubtfully. "But will Signy count her brother avenged? And surely some will denounce me for letting the dragons go unscathed. They will say we are not done with dragons—that they will return." He stopped, pricked by another question. "*Will* they?" he asked. "Will they return?"

"No!" I said quickly—too quickly—for Orrik quirked an ironic brow. "Or . . . I don't think so. Why should they? It's too perilous for them here." But in truth I was not certain even whether they would reach the land with fire beneath the earth, much less if they would stay there. And another thing occurred to me.

Eggs. There were eggs laid up all over this land in the dragons' ancient lairs. This I had surmised from the dragons' rumbling colloquies. The eggs took many years to hatch—how many I did not know. And milk. Baby dragons drank milk. So the mothers at least must return.

"Mmm," Orrik said again, eyeing me closely. "I *could* . . . erect a fortress here, on this island, to guard against the dragons' return. And I could name it . . . Rog. Or rather, I would name the island Rog, and the fortress, the castle of Rog." The king nodded as if to himself. "He would like that, to have a fortress named for him. And," he added shrewdly, "it would sap the venom from those who would make of him a saint and rebel against me in his name.

"Yes." Orrik began to pace. "Yes, that's what I'll do. I can bring Signy around—the dragons are gone, and who else is there for her? And you will return to your home steading a living legend. And I will be the wise king who ordered it all—"

"Your grace," I interrupted. "I no longer wish to go home. I want to stay at your steading, helping Corwyn in the mews."

"At my steading? In the *mews*? I am making a *legend* of you, Kara, and legends don't drudge in a steading mews!"

"I have done so all this winter."

"But you are not ever . . . biddable," he said. "I give you orders; you go your own way. How am I to trust you underfoot?"

"How will you trust me apart?"

Orrik sighed, then squinted at me thoughtfully. "Perhaps," he said, "if you had some distraction . . ." A smile slowly spread across his face. "Kazan!" he shouted. "Approach!"

Kazan trotted across the snow toward us.

"Will you build me a ship or no?" Orrik demanded. "I need to know *now*!"

Kazan flicked a puzzled glance at me, then looked back at the king. "Ah, your grace—"

"Let me put it to you thus," Orrik said. "If you will stay and build me a ship, Kara may bide at the steading, under my protection, for as long as she wills. If not, she must leave. So, Kazan. Perhaps I may yet get a ship out of you?"

Kazan turned deliberately from Orrik to me, gazed full into my eyes. I felt the warmth rise up and flood my face. I was smiling like a fool.

"Perhaps," Kazan said slowly, not moving his eyes from my own, "perhaps you may."

Gudjen went round the bathhouse lighting torches while I stripped off my clothes and pulled the bath tunic over my head. We had put in to the steading late the night before. I had stayed up even later, allowing Orrik to treat me as a legend amid the hubbub of questions and tidings. Gudjen had let me sleep far into the morning, for once. But the moment I had wakened she was there, poking her head between my bedcurtains. "Might we see," she had asked, "what tells in the steam?"

A request, not an order.

Something new.

But I, too, wished to see.

Now Gudjen began pouring water over the hot stones. Steam hissed, billowed up into the rafters in seething coils. The air lay heavy in my lungs, swirled thick and white before me.

And then it began. Steam and smoke gathered above in a single, roiling mass. A figure began to form: huge and smoky-dark. And then . . . there was Byrn, regarding me from above.

She brought her massive head down beside me—so close, so clear that I saw myself mirrored on the surface of her eye. I blinked. The steam dragon blinked. And my mirror image turned, moved away from me. No. It was *not* my image, I saw, but the image of another—a girl I had never seen—one with a mass of yellow hair plaited long behind her back.

She seemed to walk *into* the dragon eye to where an old woman sat at a claywheel. There was something . . . known about this woman. Something about her eyes . . . The claywheel began to spin. The clay whirled, rose up, formed into a smooth, round object: an egg. Then all at once it cracked; sharp creatures sprang up out of it.

Dragons. Baby dragons.

They thinned, grew faint. And all was breaking up

now—the woman, the girl, the dragon—dissolving into droplets of mist. But I thought I felt something, a voice shuddering
through my bones:

<If a girl with green eyes calls, we will come.>

And Gudjen was raising the smokehole cover, setting the
door ajar.

I breathed in the cool air, wiped away the sweat that
trickled into my eyes.

A hatching.

The dragons *would* come back, I knew it. But the rest of
it—the girl, the old woman, the clay—what was that?

"Did you," Gudjen began, and for the first time I felt
uncertainty in her voice, "understand—"

I was spared answering, for the door flew wide and a small
figure came bursting through. It was Myrra, with Rath behind
her. She hurtled into my arms, nearly knocking me down. I
clasped her to me, laughing, then tucked her under one arm
and hugged Rath with the other. I fussed over his bandaged
shoulder—for too long, Myrra deemed. She tickled me to draw
my notice. I swung her up over my head and down again,
provoking gales of giggles.

It was then that I saw.

The old woman's eyes . . . were *Myrra's* eyes—wrinkled
and old, but somehow the same.

"Kara?" Myrra asked, suddenly somber. "What's amiss?"

"Nothing," I said, then drew her and Rath to me again.
I held them close, knowing there was yet more work to do,
and that they would aid me in it.

Epilogue

Here there be dragons.

—INSCRIPTION
AT EDGE OF
KRAGISH
MAP

Late in the day the ceremony begins, with a clash of swords on shields within the fortress. We are assembled on the highland without. The council bluff, as now they call it. There are many of us; folk voyage to the island of Rog from the far reaches of the kingdom each autumn, for reunions with old friends, for trade, for the spectacle.

"Time for you to play the legend again and ruin another good gown," Kazan said irreverently this morning when we parted. I laugh softly now, remembering. Elve, our eldest daughter, looks questioningly up at me. I smile, put my arm around her. Then Bjerka, her sister, scoots in close, not wanting to be left out of a hug.

We are seated on a bench near the king and Signy and

their three sons. Gudjen has taken firm control of the princes: Jorik, the heir, and Hakar, his younger brother. A nurse cares for the third, the infant, Urk.

Signy produced her sons forthwith, as was her duty, and then considered her obligation met. She spends her days making the grand castle in the south ever grander—keeping the masons and the smiths and the weavers of the region well employed.

Now the Sentinels, their shadows stretching long before them, file out from the fortress gate and onto the grounds. They wear the red capes and copper armbands of their order. Last of all come the three white-cloaked youths who will be sworn in this day.

Orrik mounts the dais to make his speech. It is a long one—it always is—interspersed with bursts of cheering. Urk, in his nurse's arms, begins to fret. My daughters squirm and whisper. But the king's elder sons, in Gudjen's charge, sit still as stones.

Orrik tells of the dragon kyn's flight, seven years past. His own part in the tale increases with each passing year, and the dragons grow more fierce. This pleases the folk. Ever Orrik pleases the folk.

My gaze drifts out over the sea, to where Skava led the dragons. Even on this, the clearest of days, I can see no land to the north. It is beyond the curve of the horizon, Kazan tells me whenever I ask.

I have sought for Skava in the autumn migrations each year, have sat through innumerable steam-workings to discover how she fared. But the steam never showed more of her, nor of the dragons.

She never returned.

I sigh. It is an old loss. I'm accustomed to it now. Still, memory tugs at me. . . .

But my attention has lapsed, for now the crier calls, "Landerath!" and Rath steps to the fore. I catch the flash of something on his chest, the amulet Myrra gave him before she and Corwyn departed for their homeland. Rath is the last and youngest of the initiates, although, at fifteen, he is counted a man grown.

The youths recite their vows. They kneel before Orrik to receive armbands and cloaks.

And now Rath is forsworn. For in private he has vowed to help the dragons—not slay them—when they return for the hatching. He will join us in our plans, all of us who secretly prepare the way.

Rath passes before the cheering crowd, stopping briefly before me. He nods gravely. I nod back, knowing the price he has paid in forswearing himself, yet knowing also that the danger and loneliness of his chosen course matter little to him. I wonder if ever they will. I wonder if ever he will begrudge my drawing him into my schemes.

And now it is time for my part, the ceremonial calling of doves.

It is all staged, of course. I walk to the dais, glancing briefly up at the window in the tower where the doves are kept. The only difficulty is not sending my call too far, for then other birds would come and spoil the effect.

Orrik signals with a chopping motion.

I hold out my arms. I call: <Come.>

Silence, broken only by the roar of surf, the snap and crack of pennants in the wind. Then they explode from the tower window: a cloud of white doves, wings fluttering and creaking in the air, stray feathers drifting gently down like snow. The birds float down to alight upon me: my head, my shoulders, my arms. They hook their claws into my gown: a heavy, living mantle of doves.

Then . . . something else . . . I feel something. . . .

I look sharply up and see her in the sky, swooping down toward me.

Startled, I let go of the doves with my mind. They scatter in panic before the falcon. She glides through them but does not pursue them; she is coming for me. She stalls, pitches up, alights with a *thunk* upon my wrist.

Skava.

I know her as I would know the face of one of my brothers.

She is older now, by seven years, and shows it. Her beak is cracked; her wing markings have faded to gray; a talon is missing from one foot. I wonder how that happened. I wonder what life she has lived. She turns, regards me with her keen black eyes; I feel the thin, cold ripple of her consciousness.

My heart is full.

"It's *time* you came home," I murmur. I hesitate to touch her yet; she might consider me presumptuous.

"Pssst!" Gudjen is hissing at me, gesturing furiously at the doves.

Reluctantly I drag my attention from Skava and set about calling the wayward birds. It is toilsome this time, for I must overcome their objections to a falcon on my fist. But doves are foolish and biddable. At last they light down on me again. A gull or two joins them, but I doubt that any save for Gudjen will object.

Then at another signal from the king, I release them. They sail away across the sea, an echo of when I sent the dragons to the northern land. But I know that Kazan is whistling for them in the knarr, with food to tempt them and empty crates for taking them home. They are obedient; I trained them well.

Skava stares after them but does not follow. Shyly, I move to scratch her feet—now bright yellowish-orange with age.

She fluffs her feathers, makes a burbling noise in her throat, and then begins to preen.